Warwickshire County Council

B ED			
1/14			

This item is to be returned or renewed before the latest date above. It may be borrowed for a further period if not in demand. **To renew your books:**

- **Phone the 24/7 Renewal Line 01926 499273 or**
- **Visit www.warwickshire.gov.uk/libraries**

Discover • Imagine • Learn • *with libraries*

Warwickshire
County Council

"Will keep you turning the pages."
— *Forbes*

"Compulsively readable."
— *National Review*

D1423570

013953285 6

"Are they so fascinating?" the girl in the pink bikini asked.

"What?" Ross said.

"My breasts. You're staring at them."

"They're very nice."

"Thank you," she said. She adjusted the bikini halter and lay back on the sand. "Is that a professional judgment?"

At that moment, an excited little man came running up to Ross. His eyes moved furtively up and down the beach as he talked.

"Doctor!" he said breathlessly. "Come with me, please. We must talk."

"Now?" He looked at the girl. "I'm busy now."

"No, no, it is urgency. I must talk with you. Now." He tugged at Ross's arm. "Please, come. Come!"

They began to walk down the beach to the water.

"Doctor," the man said in a low voice, "you must not do it. You must not."

"What are you talking about?" Ross thought for a moment that he was talking about the girl, telling him to avoid the girl. But that was crazy. "How do you know I'm a doctor?"

"Doctor," the Spaniard said, lowering his voice, "you must not do the autopsy."

"What autopsy?"

The man waved his hand irritably. "Please, Doctor, there is not the time. I come as a friend, to warn you. Do not do the autopsy."

"I don't know what you're talking about," Ross said.

"Listen," he hissed, his voice low and harsh. "If you do the autopsy, we will kill you..."

ZERO COOL

by Michael Crichton

WRITING AS JOHN LANGE

A HARD CASE CRIME NOVEL

A HARD CASE CRIME BOOK

(HCC-MC4)

First Hard Case Crime edition so credited: November 2013

Published by

Titan Books
A division of Titan Publishing Group Ltd
144 Southwark Street
London SE1 0UP

in collaboration with Winterfall LLC

ZERO COOL™
by Michael Crichton writing as John Lange™

ISBN 978-1-78329-121-2

Design direction by Max Phillips
www.maxphillips.net

Typeset by Swordsmith Productions

The name "Hard Case Crime" and the Hard Case Crime logo
are trademarks of Winterfall LLC. Hard Case Crime books
are selected and edited by Charles Ardai.

Printed in the United States of America

Visit us on the web at www.HardCaseCrime.com

VIDEO INTERVIEW

"Are you comfortable, Grandpa?"

Wincing at the term, Peter Ross sat back in the chair and stared at his grandson Todd, who was eleven and held a small video camera pressed to his face. "I'm fine, Todd." Peter Ross cleared his throat. They were sitting in his summer house on Cape Cod. The whole family was there for the weekend, his son James and his daughter Emily, and their kids. Including his eldest grandson.

"This is a video interview with my grandfather, Dr. Peter Ross, who is the head of radiology at the Boston Memorial Hospital. Are you ready?"

"Yes, Todd. You can begin any time." Outside, he heard the children laughing, running down the lawn to the beach. He would rather be outside than doing this, but it was a school project for Todd, and he had promised weeks ago to do it.

"I want to ask you," Todd said, "about your early career in medicine."

"It'd be pretty boring," Peter Ross said. "I had fairly ordinary training as a young radiologist, back in the sixties."

"That's not what I heard."

"What do you mean?"

"I mean, what about your first professional paper? The one you were giving at a conference in Spain…"

Ross frowned. "How'd you hear about that?"

"When was it?"

"It was back in 1967."

"Whoa. How old were you back then?"

"*About twenty-six.*"

"*Is it true you nearly got killed by gangsters?*"

"*Not exactly.*" He hadn't thought about those days for years, now. They seemed part of some other life, it was so long ago.

"*And some dead Arab guy? The police accused you of murdering him?*"

"*Where'd you hear that?*"

"*Dad told me.*"

"*He got it wrong.*"

"*Okay,*" Todd said, "*then what really happened?*"

Ross shook his head. "*It's hard to explain,*" he said. "*I was very cocky back then, I thought I knew everything. I didn't take anything seriously. I had just finished intense study for my specialty boards, I was very tired, and I decided to take a vacation for a month. In those days, the swinging place for a young person to go was the resorts in the south of Spain.*"

"*So you went there?*" Todd said.

"*I did.*"

"*For hot babes?*"

"*I was twenty-six.*"

"*So even though you were old, you were still chasing babes?*"

Peter Ross smiled. "*That's right.*"

"*Clubbing?*"

"*We called them discos.*"

The video camera whirred. "*And how did you get in trouble with the police?*"

Peter Ross said, "*That's a long story.*"

"*And you almost got killed?*

"*From the moment I arrived in Spain,*" Ross said, "*things were very dangerous.*" He sighed. "*I found myself with a girl who thought I was a square, and said I had zero cool…*"

Part I

"Radiologists see things in black and white."
D. D. McGowan, M.D.

PROLOGUE
THE SEVENTH FLOOR

The skull had been smashed in five places. Both cheekbones were broken across the zygomatic arch; there was a fracture of the left parietal bone; the mandible was shattered near the joint; and the nose was broken in two places.

Peter Ross, sitting in the dark room on the seventh floor where the X-rays were read, stared at the plate. With him was Jackson, the plastic surgeon.

"Hell of a mess," Ross said. "You going to fix him tonight?"

"If we can. He's still unconscious. But what do you expect? They had to cut him out of the car."

"Good luck," Ross said. He pulled the X-ray of the head off the lighted, frosted glass and handed it to Jackson. "You'll be up all night."

"I know," Jackson said. "But we have to do it now. He hasn't got much of a face at the moment, you know. He looks caved in."

Ross shook his head. Maniacs, the way they drove. Taking so many chances. Sooner or later, they all got caught. "Was he drinking?"

"He certainly smelled like it." Jackson collected the X-rays and slipped them into the folder. "I'd better get down to the OR. They're prepping him now. By the way, I understand you're leaving."

"Yes," Ross said, flicking off the light box.

"Passed your radiology boards?"

Ross nodded.

"Congratulations. Where are you going?"

"Right now," Ross said, "I'm going to the annual meeting of the American Society of Radiologists."

"Oh? Where?"

"Barcelona." Ross grinned.

"You bastard. How long?"

"The conference lasts a week. But I'm staying a month."

"Going to the Costa Brava?"

"Yes."

"Before, or afterward?"

"Well, both, actually," Ross said, grinning wider. "I need a rest."

"You won't get one there," Jackson said. "It's full of English and Swedish girls, this time of year."

"Is it?" Ross said innocently. "I hadn't heard that."

"I'll bet you hadn't."

They left the radiology laboratory, walking toward the elevators. It was late at night; there was no one around.

"I hear," Jackson said conversationally, "that the girls are on the beach so thick you practically can't find any sand."

"I'll look into it."

"I hear," Jackson said, "that they are wildly eager to meet any young man, no matter how lacking in charm."

"Lucky for me."

"I hear," Jackson sighed, "that they are all deeply passionate, fabulously attractive, and incredibly sexy."

"I'll get to the bottom of these stories," Ross said.

The elevator came. Jackson punched the button for three; Ross pressed the ground floor.

"Tell me," Jackson said. "Are you going to do anything else while you're in Spain, aside from hitting the discos every night?"

"Well, yes, actually," Ross said. "I'm delivering a paper at the conference."

"You're kidding. On what?"

"Differential diagnosis of intestinal obstruction in infants."

"Unbelievable. Where did you ever find time to write a paper? You've been with that nurse on the sixth floor—"

"Pediatric nurse," Ross said, "and very helpful."

"You don't take anything seriously, do you."

"Not if I can help it."

"This is where I get out," Jackson said. The elevator doors opened on the third floor. Ahead were the swinging doors that led to the operating rooms. Jackson paused and looked back at Ross.

"I hope this trip matures you."

"Doubtful."

Ross grinned again, and took the elevator to the ground floor, walked briskly out to the parking lot, and got into his car. He drove home to his apartment and packed quickly, whistling to himself.

It was the evening of Friday, July 13th.

1. TOSSA DEL MAR

The first day was difficult. He spent too long in the sun, got a bad sunburn, and he slept poorly that night. He kept awaking with a recurrent dream—he was being paged on the hospital loudspeaker. It was an acute emergency, and he was being paged, but he could not rouse himself to answer it. He woke five times during the night, each time reaching for the phone at his bedside. Once, he even lifted up the phone and said hurriedly, "This is Dr. Ross. What's the trouble?"

There was a long silence, and then a startled Spanish voice said, "*Señor*? Trouble?"

"Never mind. I'm sorry."

He hung up and lay in bed, thinking how difficult it was to relax. After four years of constant hospital routine, it was hard to come out and just lie in the sun. Hard to live without responsibility, night calls, sleepless evenings, and groggy mornings. He was a masochist, that was the trouble. He had carefully trained himself over four years to expect difficulty, tribulation, pain.

Now he was being deprived. Hell of a thing, to take a vacation and feel deprived. He found himself trying to worry about something. But there was nothing to worry about. He was in Spain, three thousand miles from his hospital, his work, his life. No one knew him here, and no one cared.

If he could just relax, he would be fine. He might, he thought, even learn to enjoy it.

On the morning of the second day, as he was leaving the hotel, the manager stopped him.

"Dr. Ross?"

"Yes."

"Are you expecting a visitor?"

"A visitor? No."

"Because there was a man to see you last night. At least, I think he came to see you."

"What kind of a man?"

"An American. Very distinguished, with silver hair. Very cultured gentleman."

"What did he say?"

The manager looked confused. "Well, he came here, to the desk, and he said, 'Where is the doctor here?' I thought at first he might be hurt, but he was not. So I said, 'Which doctor?' because we have two; there is also a French surgeon from Arles. And he said, 'The American doctor.' "

"And?"

"And I said he must mean Dr. Ross, and he said that was exactly who he meant."

"And then?"

"Then he did a curious thing. He thanked me, and he left. A very polite and cultured gentleman."

"Did he give his name?"

"No," the manager said. "He said that he would contact you."

Probably something about the paper he was to deliver at the conference next week, Ross thought. He nodded. "All right. If he comes again, ask him to leave a message. I'll be gone most of the day."

"You are going to the beach, sir?"

"That's right," Ross said. "I'm going to the beach."

❄

The beach at Tossa del Mar would never win any prizes. The sand was dirty, coarse, and grating; there was trash everywhere, empty bottles, paper cups, unfinished food; the wind blew in hot and stifling from the sea.

But then, the beach at Tossa was barely visible for the girls. Jackson had been right: they were everywhere. Packed side by side, heavily oiled, bodies glistening in the sun. There were Swedish girls, French girls, Italian girls, and English girls; there were tall girls and short girls, slim girls and ample girls; there were girls in small bikinis, and girls in smaller bikinis, and girls in practically nothing at all; there were girls blonde and brunette, sexy and sweet, plain and pretty.

And hardly a man in sight.

It was, Ross thought, almost too good to be true. He walked along the water's edge, drinking beer from a bottle, feeling very good. Some of the girls were looking at him directly, and some were pretending not to look at him, but really were. Not that it mattered. Not that it mattered at all.

And then, he saw one girl who was truly spectacular, black-haired and long-legged, wearing a shocking pink bikini. Her eyes were closed to the hot sun; she seemed to be asleep. He walked over to her and bent over, admiring the view, and then his sunglasses, slippery with tanning lotion, fell with a soft plop onto her smooth abdomen.

She opened her eyes, which were clear blue, and looked at him. Then she picked up the sunglasses.

"Are these for me?"

"Well, uh…no, not exactly."

She shrugged and gave them back to him. "You should be more careful."

"I'll remember that."

"The next girl might keep them. And then where would you be?"

"Out of a pair of sunglasses."

"And into a stifling hot romance with some travel agency secretary. You'd never escape alive."

"It sounds awful," he grinned.

"You'll learn."

She looked at him again, her eyes moving over his face. "You're a doctor," she said.

He was surprised. "How did you know?"

"Doctors always look clean." She pointed to the bottle of beer in his hand. "Is that cold?"

He nodded. She reached for it and took a swallow. He continued to stand, uncertain.

"As long as you're trying to pick me up," she said, "you might as well sit down and be comfortable."

He sat. She took another swallow and handed the bottle back to him. She wiped her mouth with the back of her hand.

"Are they so fascinating?" she asked.

"What?"

"My breasts. You're staring at them."

"They're very nice."

"Thank you," she said. She adjusted the bikini halter and lay back on the sand. "Is that a professional judgment?"

"Not exactly," he said.

"Are you on vacation?"

"Yes."

"Married?"

"No."

"Then we have something in common," the girl said. "Tell me about yourself."

He shrugged. "Nothing much to tell. My name is Peter Ross, I'm a radiologist from America, I have just passed my specialty boards, and I have not seen the outside of a hospital for four years. Now I am in sunny Spain for a month, where I intend to lie in the sun and do absolutely nothing."

"Except pick up girls."

"If possible," he nodded.

"Oh, it's possible. You may have noticed how possible it is." She looked at him. "You have a nice smile. I like American smiles. They're so wholesome. May I have some more of that beer?"

He gave her the bottle.

"I suppose you want to know about me," she said. "Angela Locke. English. Unhappy childhood. Stewardess. Also on vacation."

She passed the bottle back, empty. She reached into her purse for cigarettes, lit one, and looked at him. "How many pairs of sunglasses have you lost doing that little trick?"

"It wasn't a trick. It was an accident."

"I see." She smiled.

"But as long as I'm picking you up," he said, "shall we have lunch together?"

"Of course."

"And dinner?"

"Perhaps." She gave him a slow smile. "If you still want to."

"Oh, I'll want to."

"I'm very expensive," she said. "Sure you want to get involved?"

"I'll take my chances."

At that moment, an excited, dark-skinned little Spaniard came running up to Ross. He wore jeans and a cheap shirt; his feet were bare. His eyes moved furtively up and down the beach as he talked.

"Doctor!" he said breathlessly. "Thank the God I found you!"

Ross had never seen the man before. "Is something wrong?"

"Wrong? No. Nothing is wrong. Come with me, please. We must talk."

"Now?" He looked at the girl. "I'm busy now."

"No, no, it is urgency. I must talk with you. Now." He spoke hurriedly, with a thick Spanish accent. His eyes never stopped scanning the beach. He tugged at Ross's arm. "Please, come. Come!"

"Where?"

"Just down the beach. It will not be long."

Ross hesitated, then stood. He said to the girl, "Excuse me a minute."

The girl had watched everything with lazy eyes. She did not seem surprised, and merely shrugged.

"Will you be here when I get back?" Ross said.

"Probably," she said, lying back in the sun, closing her eyes.

The little man tugged at his arm, "Come, Doctor, come."

"All right," Ross said.

They began to walk down the beach to the edge of the water. It was the hottest part of the day; children played in the surf while nursemaids stood and watched; a pair of solemn girls in bikinis gravely tested the water with manicured toes. The little man walked alongside Ross, excited, hopping from one foot to the other.

"Doctor," he said in a low voice, "you do not know what you are getting in for."

"What?"

"Doctor, you must not do it. You must not."

"What are you talking about?" He thought for a moment that he was talking about the girl, telling him to avoid the girl. But that was crazy. "How do you know I'm a doctor?"

"Doctor, it will be better if you left Spain immediately."

"*What?*"

"Yes, you must," the Spaniard said gravely. "You must."

"But I just arrived."

"Yes, but you must," the Spaniard repeated.

"Why?"

"Because."

"Because what?"

"Because," the Spaniard said, lowering his voice, *"you must not do the autopsy."*

"What autopsy?"

The man waved his hand irritably. "Please, Doctor, there is not the time. I come as a friend, to warn you. Do not do the autopsy."

"I don't know what you're talking about," Ross said. He was becoming annoyed. An agitated lunatic prancing down the beach, telling him to leave Spain, telling him about some goddamned autopsy. For Christ's sake: he hadn't seen an autopsy since his days as a medical student.

"This is concerning great seriousness," the man said. "Much is at stake. I wish you to swear you will not do the autopsy."

"What autopsy?" Ross said again.

"You will be the fool if you do it," the little man said. "No matter what they offered you."

"Nobody offered me anything."

"Listen," he hissed, his voice low and harsh. "If you do the autopsy, we will kill you. Do you understand? Kill you."

And with that, he walked off irritably, hurrying away from the water, back toward the town. Peter Ross stood astonished and watched him go.

"What was that all about?" Angela said.

"Damned if I know. He kept raving about an autopsy. I mustn't do an autopsy." Ross dropped down and stretched out on the sand, lying on his back in the sun.

"The Spaniards are all insane," she said. "You'll learn that sooner or later. It was probably a mistake."

"It must be," Ross said. "Because I'm not qualified to do autopsies. I'm a radiologist, not a pathologist."

"And I'm hungry," Angela said. She stood and brushed sand from her long legs. "When are you taking me to lunch?"

He grinned up at her. "You don't beat around the bush."

"People who beat around the bush," she said, "are afraid to get into the thick of things."

"You have a dirty mind."

"I have an empty stomach," she said. "When are we going to lunch?"

"Now," he said, getting up quickly. "Right now."

2. THE PALLBEARERS

It was nearly four when he returned to his hotel room, relaxed from the sun, the good food at lunch, and the wine. He was meeting Angela again at six for drinks before dinner. He felt good as he stripped off his bathing trunks and took a hot shower to wash off the sand from the beach.

This was the way things ought to be, he thought. Hot sun, spicy food, and engaging women. And no work: that was very important, no work.

There was a knock at the door just as he climbed out of the shower. He wrapped the towel around his waist and answered it. Four men stood outside in the hall. They were grave, dressed in dark, somber suits, and each wearing a black armband. One of them, a tall man with graying hair, seemed to be the spokesman.

"Dr. Ross?"

"Yes."

"Have we come at an inconvenient time?"

Ross looked down at the towel around his waist. "Well, actually…"

"Please forgive us for doing so," the man said smoothly, entering the room. The other three followed. "But this is a matter of utmost urgency."

Ross shut the door, feeling strange. "Won't you sit down?"

"Thank you," the man said. "My name is Robert Carrini, Dr. Ross. These men are my cousins: George, Ernest, and Samuel."

The four men nodded toward Ross politely. Ross nodded back and tightened the towel around his waist. The leader, Robert Carrini, did not seem to notice the towel. He had an immaculate, cultured air; he might have been the curator of a museum or the president of a bank.

"What can I do for you?" Ross said.

"We come," Carrini said, "at a time of tragedy. Great, heart-rending tragedy." He touched his armband absently. "It is difficult to find the words to explain. This has been a shock for all of us."

"I'm sorry," Ross said, not knowing what else to say.

"There has been a death," Carrini said. "My dear brother. In Barcelona. It was very sudden, a great shock."

"What happened?"

"He died violently," Carrini said slowly. "My brother always led a violent life, and he died a violent death. We all knew it would happen one day. He was an unhappy, confused young man, and we knew how it would end. But that is not much help when the day finally arrives. So sudden." He shook his head. "So sudden."

Ross paused a moment, then said, "Why have you come to me?"

Carrini started to answer, but could not. He dropped his head and began to sob silently, his body shaking.

One of the others came forward, rested a hand on Carrini's shoulder, and said, "You must excuse Robert. He has still not accepted this, in his own mind. He was very close to his brother, you see. It was hard on him. Doctor, his brother was not a good man. There was trouble all his life."

"I see."

"Now, with all the legal technicalities…" The cousin shrugged.

Ross still did not understand. He waited. "The problem," the man said, "involves taking Stephano back to America, the country he loved."

"Why should that be a problem?"

"He was asked to leave America, five years ago. There are technicalities."

"Asked to leave? You mean deported?"

"It had to do," said the man carefully, "with an income tax dispute. The government wished to discredit him, so they accused him of not paying taxes. A lie, of course. But they sent him away. Stephano loved America, Doctor. He always said he wished to be buried there. Next to his mother, God rest her soul."

"I see," Ross said.

"We do not know who shot him yesterday in Barcelona," the man continued. "It does not matter. The police will not search for his killer. The Spanish also considered Stephano undesirable."

Stephano sounded like everyone's favorite, Ross thought. He said nothing.

"We have come to Spain to take his body back to America. This is permitted, but first, there are many technicalities. Many rules and regulations."

"Such as?"

"First," the man said, "there must be an autopsy."

Ross suddenly felt cold. "An autopsy? Why?"

The man shrugged. "It is the law."

"Won't the Spanish authorities perform it?"

At this moment, Robert Carrini seemed to pull himself together. He wiped his eyes with a handkerchief and said, "No, that is not the problem. In order to return to America, the autopsy must be performed by an American doctor."

Ross frowned. It all sounded very peculiar. "Wouldn't you be better off working through the Embassy in Madrid?"

Robert sighed patiently. "We have tried. They will not help us. They will not lift a finger. They would like to forget that my brother ever existed. They do not want him to return to America—even dead."

There was a short pause. Robert Carrini shook his head again.

"I could not believe it," he said, "when I talked to them. They would have blocked his return to America if they could. Fortunately, they cannot. The law permits it. But they have raised every obstacle. For instance, an autopsy by the Spanish police would be valid if papers were authorized by the American consul in Barcelona. But he will not. Nor will he help find an American doctor. He will do nothing."

"So you came to me."

"Yes. We found a doctor in Madrid who works with the Embassy, but he refused. We searched everywhere for another. But it is so difficult…"

"Couldn't you ship the body back and have the autopsy performed in America?"

"No. Not allowed. It must be performed here in Spain."

Ross shrugged. "I would like to help you," he said, "that goes without saying. But frankly, I am not qualified. I am a radiologist, not a pathologist. I have attended autopsies, but never performed one."

Robert waved his hand impatiently. "You possess a doctorate of medicine?"

"Yes."

"You are qualified to practice?"

"Radiology, yes."

"Then it does not matter. The law says that a duly certified

American physician must perform the postmortem. It does not stipulate a pathologist."

"But gentlemen—"

"We need your help, Doctor Ross," said Ernest, very firmly. "You must help us. You must help us return Stephano to America."

"I would like to, of course, but—"

"This is a matter of great importance to me, to my family, to my poor father, who is eighty-seven and slowly dying of cancer. I appeal to you—as a *doctor*."

Ross shook his head. "I'm very sorry."

"We realize that this is an imposition on you, professionally," Carrini said. "But we hope you will make the sacrifice. As one human being to another. As one—"

"Really, I—"

"If you perform the autopsy," Carrini said, "we are prepared to pay you twenty thousand dollars."

There was a silence in the room. Ross paused, frowning. Their story had sounded peculiar; now, it seemed almost sinister. That was a lot of money for an autopsy. A hell of a lot of money.

"You are generous, but—"

"Thirty thousand."

"No, really—"

"Then fifty." Robert Carrini spat out the words. "You can see it is important to us."

Ross felt suddenly frightened. It was too much, incredibly too much. "I'm sorry. I can't."

"If I could afford more than fifty thousand dollars," Robert said, "I would pay it. I would pay a hundred or two hundred thousand to see Stephano buried in his homeland. The homeland which treated him so cruelly, so unfairly."

Ross shook his head. "I'm sorry, gentlemen."

"Doctor." Robert stood and looked hard at Ross. "*You must.*"

"I'm sorry."

"You will not reconsider?"

"No."

"Then we are lost." Carrini sighed and turned to the others. They stood and filed silently out the door. Carrini was the last to leave.

"Please," he said. "Please reconsider."

Ross shook his head.

"Then may you rot in hell," Carrini said, and slammed the door shut.

Outside, in the hall, the men removed their black armbands. One of them said to Carrini, "What do you think?"

"Very successful," Carrini said. "He will be fine. You say he has no family?"

"None."

"And he is here purely for a vacation? No friends, no relatives with him?"

"None."

"Then if something should go wrong, it will be very simple," Carrini said. "Perhaps a drowning—his body will wash ashore weeks later." He smiled slowly. "It happens all the time."

The four walked out of the hotel.

3. DRINKS AND SYMPATHY

"My God, you look awful. Has something happened? Here, drink this."

Angela pushed her vodka and lime across the table to him. He gulped it quickly.

"That's better," she said. "You really do look awful. Been seeing ghosts?"

"Worse than that," he said. He nodded to the waiter, and ordered another round of drinks. Doubles. The A.M.A. said drinking to relieve stress was a sign of early alcoholism. But the hell with the A.M.A.

"I came to Spain," he said, "to get away from all this. I came for a vacation."

Angela nodded. She was dressed casually in purple polka dot stretch pants and a loose overblouse with a scoop neck. A very low scoop neck.

"I didn't ask for this," he said. "I want nothing to do with it."

"To do with what?" she said.

"The autopsy."

"What autopsy? You're talking nonsense. Have another drink."

The drinks came. He sipped the second, sat up, and tried to pull himself together. She watched him quietly, waiting. Finally he said, "Some men came to see me this afternoon. About an autopsy."

"Like the man on the beach?"

"Yes, but these men wanted me to do it. They offered me fifty thousand dollars."

She whistled softly. "What did you tell them?"

"I told them no," he said. "By that time, I was scared. They were very genteel sorts, very quiet and polite. But I gather he was some sort of gangster."

"Who was?"

"The one who died. Apparently he was shot in Barcelona yesterday."

She snapped her fingers. "Wait a minute," she said. "I remember reading something about that. Sit tight."

She left the bar and returned a few moments later with an English newspaper. She thumbed through it quickly and folded it back, then handed it to him.

"Here. Look at this."

Ross read the story. Stephano Carrini, forty-four, deported American. Underworld contacts. Expelled from the United States after conviction for six hundred thousand dollars in tax evasion on an illegal gambling racket. Shot dead by unknown assailant in a bar in Barcelona.

"What do you know," he said.

"He was a nasty one," Angela said. "He was in England for a while, after leaving America. He was mixed up with the hoods in Brighton. They threw him out of England as well. Something about narcotics; I don't remember. But I think you were wise," she said, "not to get involved."

Ross sipped his drink and nodded.

"Do you think they'll leave you alone now?"

"I hope so."

"So do I," she said.

He looked at her, feeling the drinks begin to hit him. She seemed genuinely worried and concerned about him; he liked that. She adjusted her blouse, and he said, "What do you call that outfit?"

"This," she said, "is a patented man-getter."

"Looks more like a coming-out party to me."

She smiled. "After spending all day at the beach, it seems silly to hide your tan." There was a short silence.

"You're staring again," she said.

"Sorry. I was thinking."

"About what?"

"About my pass."

"Pass?"

"Yes. I'm going to make a pass at you soon."

"That will be interesting," she said.

"Just warning you."

"Do I need a warning?"

"Well, you know. Prior notice, that sort of thing."

"I'll be waiting," she said.

"With open arms?"

"That depends. I don't usually like passes."

"Perhaps you'll like this one."

"Perhaps," she said.

They went into the dining room for dinner. They began with gazpacho, sprinkling the cold soup with onions, peppers, and tomatoes. Then they had *pollo con ajillo*, chicken with garlic, and a bottle of Portuguese red wine.

"My God, we're going to stink after this," Angela said.

"I don't mind."

"Neither do I." She looked at him across the table. "I like you," she said.

"I like you, too."

They exchanged a direct look, and then she turned away and began eating again.

"I don't really mean that," she said. "Just forget it. Too much wine."

"It's all right."

"Don't push. I hate pushy men."

He said nothing more for a time; she seemed depressed. Over dessert, however, her spirits improved, and when they returned to the bar for brandy and coffee, she seemed happy and bubbling.

"Promise me," she said as they entered the bar, "that you won't make a pass here. I hate passes in bars."

"You seem to hate lots of things tonight."

"Not really."

"Where should I make my pass?"

"Someplace private," she said.

They sat down. The brandies came. They had a round, ordered another. While they were waiting for them, he said, "We could have them in my room."

She smiled. "We could have them here."

"There's an excellent view from my balcony."

"But it's dark."

"I could show you my etchings."

"I never look at the etchings of strange men."

The drinks came.

"We could walk along the beach."

"It's against the law to do it in public," she said. "Besides, the sand…"

He leaned over and whispered in her ear. "If you come to my room," he said, "I'll tell you a joke. Privately."

"A good one?"

"The best."

"I detest bad jokes. All that waiting, and no punch line."

"This one has a good punch line."

"Does it take long to tell?"

"That depends."

"Is it worth waiting for?"

"Definitely."

She said, "I don't know. I've heard some pretty bad jokes in my time."

"From men with no sense of humor," he said.

She smiled. "Will I laugh very hard?"

"You will be convulsed with laughter."

"It sounds like an awfully good joke."

"It is, it is."

She finished her brandy and set it down. "Then what are we waiting for?"

The room was dark, warm, and close. She sighed and rubbed up against him. He put his arm around her shoulder, and she placed her head next to his. He smelled her hair, her skin, her perfume.

"Want to hear another one?"

She smiled contentedly. "Not right now. I'm all laughed out. I didn't know doctors were like that. I mean your sense of humor."

"I'm an exception to the rule."

"I'll say." She snuggled up against him.

Half an hour later, she was sleeping peacefully. The phone rang. Ross, on the side of sleep, answered it.

"Hello?"

"Dr. Ross. This is Robert Carrini."

"Yes."

"About our little conversation today. You neglected to mention you had spoken with someone previously."

"Previously?"

"Yes. On the beach. You spoke with a man. What did he offer you?"

"Nothing. Nothing at all."

"Whatever he offered, we will match, and increase by twenty percent. Is that satisfactory?"

"Really, he didn't—"

"Dr. Ross. This is no time for foolishness. I intend that you shall perform the autopsy on my brother. There is no alternative."

"I'm sorry."

"So am I. I regret to inform you that should you continue to refuse, or attempt to leave Spain, we will be forced to kill you."

Ross said nothing.

"Is my meaning clear?"

"Quite clear."

"Good night, then."

The phone was dead.

He lay in bed, awake, for a very long time. He wondered what he had done to deserve this, and he wondered if it were some kind of elaborate practical joke cooked up by the other radiologists attending the conference, and he finally decided it was probably not a joke at all.

In the middle of the night, he awoke. Angela, sleepy-eyed and soft, was shaking his shoulder.

"What's the matter?" he said.

"You were lying in bed moaning," she said, "and gnashing your teeth."

He shivered. His body was coated in sweat. "I was dreaming," he said, "that everybody was trying to kill me."

She smiled in the darkness. "Silly boy," she said. "You were having a nightmare."

She kissed him.

"Go back to sleep," she said.

He did.

4. A SMALL AUTOPSY

In the morning, after breakfast with Angela, he left her at the beach and walked through the town. He wanted to be alone and to think.

Tossa was a town built in layers. Along the water, the town was gay and colorful, rich with the money of tourists from a dozen nations, crammed with pretty girls and greasy men, noisy discotheques, and expensive restaurants. Farther back was a layer of hotels, quiet, whitewashed, modern.

Beyond the hotel there were no more tourists, only natives, living in tiny stucco houses clumped around narrow cobbled streets that smelled of garbage, urine, and cooking oil. Clothes hung out to dry from wrought iron balconies; fat women shouted to each other and laughed; and small children ran naked, playing hide and seek.

As Ross walked, a slim man in a plaid sport shirt appeared, carrying a towel draped over one hand. The man was dressed as a tourist but carried the towel like a waiter; it was an odd combination.

"Señor?"

Ross stopped, surprised the man would speak to him. "Yes?"

"You are Dr. Ross?"

"Yes."

"Come with me."

"I'm afraid," Ross said, "that I'm busy just now. I'm on vacation and very busy. This is the busiest vacation I've ever—"

The man touched his towel, moving the roll of cloth to show the gun underneath.

"Come with me, please."

He gestured down a side street.

Ross walked.

"You are sensible," the man said.

"I'm scared," Ross said.

"That is sensible."

"Now we are getting into a metaphysical discussion," Ross said.

"Shut up," the man said pleasantly. "Please."

They walked: down one narrow, crooked street, then down an alley, and then left down another street.

"Not much of a conversationalist, are you?"

"Shut up," the man said.

"Myself, I always prefer—"

"Shut up, or I will kill you."

"Oh. Why didn't you say so in the first place?"

He was feeling stupid, giddy and stupid and absurd, walking down the street, dodging the running children and the chickens, with a man behind him holding a gun under a towel.

They came to the end of the street and made another turn.

"Down there," the man said.

He pointed to a glistening black Rolls-Royce parked at the end of the block. The chrome shone brightly in the sunlight. They walked to it, and the man opened the rear door.

"Inside."

Ross got in and found himself sitting next to an enormous man in a cowboy suit. He was at least six and a half feet tall and must have weighed three hundred pounds. His

shirt and pants were tan leather, with fringes and pearl but-
tons. Above the string tie and collar, a hearty red face was
smiling.

"Howdy," said the man.

"Hello," Ross said. "Are you from the Pony Express?"

The man frowned. "The Pony Express? No. I'm—"

Then he stopped, and laughed. "Oh, I get it. A joke, eh?
Pony Express, eh?" He laughed heavily, his voice booming
inside the car. He slapped his knee. "That's a good one, that
is. A real good one."

"What's on your mind?" Ross said.

"Just a chat," the man said. "No reason to be alarmed. Is
there?"

"I don't know. You tell me."

"No reason, no reason at all." He chuckled easily. "Smoke?"
He held forward a pack of cigarettes: Marlboros.

"No thanks."

The cowboy shrugged, lit the cigarette and sat back.

"Well now," he said. "So you're the doctor."

"Just call me sawbones," Ross said.

The cowboy chuckled. "Got a fine sense of humor, too."

"I need it."

"That's God's truth," the cowboy said, nodding solemnly.
"Want to tell me about it?"

"About what?"

"Robert Carrini."

"I don't know anything about Carrini. Who wants to know?"

"I do," the cowboy said.

"Why?"

"I like to keep track of things."

Ross sat back and watched the cowboy smoke the cigarette.
He wasn't going to talk, not without an explanation first.

"Carrini came to see you," the cowboy said, "and asked you to do the autopsy."

"Go on," Ross said. "This is fascinating."

The cowboy stared at him for a moment, then shook his head. "Son," he said, "you can try a man's patience, you know that? Don't you understand I'm trying to *help* you?"

"No," Ross said. "I don't understand anything."

"Well, look here, son. If you're not careful, you could get killed. This is serious business. What happened when Carrini came to see you?"

Ross sighed. It was crazy. The whole damn thing was crazy. "I told him no."

"Why?"

"Somebody else had already promised to kill me if I did the autopsy."

"Who was that?"

"A man on the beach."

"Spanish man?"

"Yes."

"Short nervous-type fella?"

"Yes."

"Go on," said the cowboy in a neighborly drawl.

"So I refused when Carrini came."

"You're not doing the autopsy?"

"Well, later he called back and promised to kill me if I *didn't* do it."

"My," said the cowboy. "You're between a rock and a hard place, aren't you?"

"Yes," Ross said.

"Better take my advice," he said.

"What's that?"

"Be damned careful."

"I'll remember that."

"Yes sir, if I was you, I'd be *damned* careful."

"Anything else?"

"Yes. Have you, ah…heard anything?"

"About what?"

"About this whole business."

"No. Just that the stakes seem pretty high. Carrini offered me fifty thousand to do the autopsy."

"Cheapskate," said the cowboy. Then he frowned, thinking. "Of course, perhaps he intended to let you keep it."

Ross said nothing. The man was thinking. At length, he shook his head.

"No, impossible. He would never let you keep it."

"Why not?"

"Listen, boy, if I was you I'd really be damned careful. You're involved, you realize that."

"What should I do?"

"Do?"

"Yes. About the autopsy."

"Perform it, of course. You thinking of doing anything *else*?"

"I really wasn't sure."

"Wise up, boy. Perform that autopsy, and then get the hell out of the country." He scratched the back of his large hand reflectively. "I think we can handle everything from there. Of course, it'd be better if you didn't do the autopsy, but we can't have you getting killed, can we?"

"It doesn't strike me as a good idea."

"No, me neither. All that investigation, all those police…"

The cowboy lapsed into silence. He took a final drag on his cigarette, powered down the darkened glass window, and threw it outside.

"So nobody has told you what's going on, eh?"

"No."

"Well, that's probably best. Little knowledge is a dangerous thing, eh?" He laughed.

"I'd like to know," Ross said.

" 'Course you'd like to know. Everybody'd like to know. That's the point."

"Yes."

"Any fool can see that." The cowboy sighed. "You just go on about your business, do the autopsy, and clear out. That's best."

He nodded to the man outside with the towel. The door was opened for Ross. Ross got out, and the towel man stepped behind the wheel of the car.

The engine started. The cowboy leaned out the window and looked at Ross.

"You seem like a nice fella. Myself, I hate docs. Never could stand needles, you know? But you seem like a nice fella. Remember what I told you: be damned careful. Damned careful."

And with that, the Rolls-Royce drove off in a cloud of dry, brown dust.

Sitting at a table in an outdoor café, he ordered a triple Scotch on the rocks, though it was only ten in the morning. The waiter, a tired, sad-faced Spaniard, was sympathetic.

"Women?" he said.

"No. Thank God."

"Not women?"

He wandered off, astonished.

Ross stared at the crowds passing by, the girls in stretch pants and bikinis, the men in casual pullovers and slacks. A resort crowd, on vacation. Just like he was. Having a good time, enjoying themselves, not a care in the world.

He wondered what he should do. He could, of course, call the police. But they would never believe him. He could call the consulate in Barcelona. But they wouldn't believe him either. In fact, the more he thought about it, the more he came to realize that *nobody* would believe him.

He hardly believed it himself.

A cheerful voice alongside him said, "Good morning." He looked over and saw Carrini, dressed as he had been the day before—a dark suit, white shirt, and a silver tie. Christ, silver ties.

"I've been looking for you, Dr. Ross. Fortunately, it is a small town. I see you are already drinking."

"Yes." Ross turned the glass in his hand. "I got thirsty just now. Very, very thirsty."

"Yes," Carrini said. "The sun is quite warm, isn't it?"

"Quite warm."

Carrini smiled reassuringly. "But there is no reason to be afraid. I have good news."

"You're not going to kill me after all?"

"Please," Carrini said, raising his hand. "You must not misunderstand me. We never had any intention of killing you."

"Reassuring."

"In fact, what I wanted to tell you was that this will all be over in a few hours."

Ross frowned. "What will?"

"You see," Carrini said, "One wants to work quickly in this heat. The Spaniards, you know, do not have so much refrigeration."

"I see."

"It can be quite unpleasant, after a few days." Carrini smiled. "But that will not concern us. The body has been re-frigerated since a few hours after death. There is no problem. May I buy you another drink?"

"Why not?"

"Yes, indeed," Carrini said. "Why not?"

Half an hour later, Carrini hailed a taxi, and they both got in. Carrini gave rapid directions in Spanish.

"Where are we going?"

"You'll see."

Ross sat back in his seat. "As long as I have no choice in this matter," he said, "don't you think you ought to tell me what's going on?"

"Of course. It's quite simple. My brother was a rather unsavory character—I hate to say gangster, it sounds so melo-dramatic. He was in Spain, working at a highly lucrative business. I regret to say—" he pursed his lips disapprovingly "—that it concerned opium."

"I see."

"The opium was brought in from Bombay and Beirut and broken down here. Converted to heroin, I think. Or what-ever it is one makes from opium. In any event, it was then transported to New York. I don't know how. The conversion plant was located in the mountains north of Barcelona. It has now been destroyed."

"And then your brother was shot."

"Yes. In a bar."

"Was he working with Spaniards?"

"No. Greeks, I believe. I am searching for them now." He said it mildly and lit a cigarette.

"Why was your brother killed?"

"I do not know. As I told you before, he was a violent man."

"What's your line of work, Mr. Carrini?"

"I am an importer," he said slowly. "I deal in fine gem-stones, for the American market. It has been my work for many years. I travel a great deal and am known throughout the world." He smiled. "For my scrupulous honesty."

"I don't doubt it."

"I'm sure," Carrini said, "that you don't."

He fell silent then, leaning against the seat and staring moodily out the window. The car traveled north, away from the ocean to the foothills, and then beyond to the southern plains. The land was flat, ringed with blue mountains. It was a fertile, wheat-growing area.

The taxi continued on for several more minutes and then abruptly pulled over to the side of the road. Ross looked up in surprise. There was nothing but yellow wheatfields in every direction. Not a house, not a sign of life anywhere.

"Good," Carrini said. He paid the driver and opened the door.

"We're getting out here?" Ross said.

"That's right. Go on."

Ross got out. Inland, the heat was devastating—dry, hot, merciless. He stood with Carrini at the side of the road and watched as the taxi turned around and headed back for Tossa del Mar and the coast.

"Now what?"

"Come with me."

Carrini looked around to get his bearings, then struck off across one of the wheatfields.

"Where are we going?"

"You're full of questions today."

The wheat was crisp, dry, and waist deep. They walked several hundred yards away from the road, and then Carrini stopped.

"Here."

"In the middle of the field?"

"We're early. Have a cigarette and relax."

"I don't smoke."

"As you wish."

Carrini lit a cigarette and they stood in the field, waiting in the hot sun. Several minutes passed. Carrini ground the cigarette under his heel, then immediately lit another. He glanced around from time to time.

Ross said, "May I ask—"

"I told you. We are early."

"For what?"

Then Ross heard the sound. It came from the east, a low, thumping, pulsing sound, coming closer.

Helicopter.

Carrini checked his watch. "Right on time," he said, nodding in satisfaction.

Now they could see it in the distance, moving high, the bubble cockpit reflecting the sun. The helicopter passed over them, the shadow crossing like a dark angel; it circled, came back, hovered a few yards away, and began its descent.

The wind was fierce, whistling, roaring, raising a storm of dust. Ross squinted and then closed his eyes to protect them from the dust. He coughed, the air was thick. The noise came closer, and then Carrini was tugging at him.

"Come on, come on."

They ran to the helicopter, and climbed aboard. It was a small, jet-powered model; seats for four. Another man was sitting there, in the back. As soon as Ross and Carrini were aboard, the pilot lifted off again. They all put on headphones.

Carrini turned to the man in the back and said, "Where is Martin?"

"Waiting for us. At the hospital."

"He has it?"

"Yes."

Carrini nodded. "And who is with him?"

"He…he is alone."

For a moment, Carrini seemed angry, but then he became very calm. "Alone?" he asked.

"Yes, sir. There was a last-minute problem, a difficulty. We tried—"

"He shouldn't have been left alone," Carrini said softly.

"It was the only way…"

Carrini looked at the man, "It would be a disaster," he said, "if anything has happened."

"I'm sure nothing—"

"Let us hope so," Carrini said. He turned away and said nothing more.

Ross looked out the window at the harsh, dry landscape rushing beneath them. He tried to make some sense of the conversation, but it meant nothing to him, except that it seemed increasingly clear that Carrini was involved in his brother's heroin operation.

By looking at the sun, Ross tried to determine the direction they were flying and decided it was west and north. They flew for twenty minutes, which meant they were headed north of Barcelona. Where the heroin plant was supposed to be.

He frowned.

"Worried, Doctor?" It was Carrini.

"I told you. I've never done an autopsy before."

"I understand," Carrini said, "that they are not difficult."

Ross shrugged. "You're taking me to a hospital?"

"Yes. More or less."

A few minutes later, they came over a rocky rise, and Ross saw it. At first, he thought it was a resort—an oasis of green in the midst of the desert. Then he noticed the buildings, which were blocklike and distinctly institutional. The helicopter banked, and settled onto an even green lawn.

They got out.

Seen from the ground, the buildings around them were high, flat, and depressing.

"What is this, a penitentiary?"

Carrini laughed. "Close. A sanatorium, for tuberculosis patients whose cases are resistant to drugs. The patients are Germans, mostly. They like the climate."

Ross walked with Carrini toward the main building. They entered a broad lobby with a reception desk to one side. Overhead, an old fan spun slowly, creaking. It reminded Ross of a dilapidated hotel, once luxurious, now faded and rather sad.

A short, kindly looking man in a white uniform came up. He was bald and bespectacled, in his late fifties. He seemed to fit the surroundings, for his manner was gentle but rather melancholy.

"Ah, Dr. Garber," Carrini said. "This is Dr. Ross." To Ross, he explained, "Dr. Garber is the director of the Heitzman Sanatorium."

"How do you do," Ross said, shaking hands. Garber smiled. "So you are the pathologist," he said, in a thick German accent.

"That's right," Carrini said, with a quick glance at Ross. "Quite a stroke of luck to find a vacationing pathologist, eh?"

"Indeed, indeed," Garber said. "Very fortunate." He led the way down a corridor from the lobby. "Come along, gentlemen. You can begin immediately. Your relatives have already arrived, Mr. Carrini."

"Excellent," Carrini said.

Garber turned to Ross. "It's not often that we get a pathologist here," he said. "And I'm afraid I've fallen behind in my journals. I used to be quite interested in pathology. I even did research, for a time, on caseous necrosis. But that was many years ago. I imagine everything is different, now. I should like to talk to you about the latest findings."

"Actually, Dr. Ross is on a tight schedule," Carrini said. "He was kind to take time out to do the autopsy at all."

"Of course," Garber said.

Ross said nothing. He was worried. Garber had obviously been told that he was a pathologist; if he stayed to observe the autopsy, he would recognize immediately that he was dealing with an amateur.

"I myself am a surgeon," Garber said. "From the old days, when there was no INH and strep. But it was challenging. Thoracic surgery was so new." He sighed. "My assistant will help you with your work," he said. "I myself must make rounds in a few minutes."

"All right," Ross said.

They went down a corridor, turned, and found themselves on another. The walls were painted a drab brown; Ross found it depressing.

A girl came out of a side room. She wore a white uniform. She was tall, very blonde, and lushly proportioned.

"Herr Doktor…"

She stopped when she saw Carrini and Ross.

"Oh, excuse me, I thought you were alone."

"It's all right," Garber said. He turned to the others. "This is my assistant, Karin. Mr. Carrini, and Dr. Ross."

She nodded shyly. Then she looked at Ross, an odd, questioning, almost frightened look.

Dr. Garber said, "You will assist Dr. Ross."

"Yes, sir."

"I'm sure he won't need much help," Garber said, smiling at Ross. "Just show him where things are."

She nodded.

"We have only one autopsy room here," Garber said, "and it's not used anymore. No one dies of tuberculosis these days, except the very poor, and the poor do not come to the Heitzman Sanatorium. You may find the room a bit dusty, but I think it will be satisfactory."

"Fine," Ross said.

"Then I leave you for now. Karin will take you the rest of the way."

With a formal bow, he departed. Karin, Ross, and Carrini walked on, down still another corridor.

"How long have you been here?" Ross said to Karin.

"A year," she said. She seemed unhappy, unwilling to talk. She glanced up at him once, and her eyes still held that odd look.

At the end of the corridor were twin doors leading to an operating room. Four men—including three who had been in Ross's hotel room the night before—were waiting there, solemn-faced. The fourth was a burly man with a briefcase. All four wore business suits.

"My cousins," said Carrini when they arrived. He nodded to the double doors. "The body is there?"

"Yes," Karin said.

"Then you'd better start. I will watch."

Ross turned: "Are you sure? These things can be—"

"I will watch," Carrini said, his voice flat.

"I really don't advise—"

"We will not argue about it," Carrini said. "My mind is made up."

He nodded to the others. "They will wait outside, but I will watch."

"All right," Ross said. He could not imagine anyone wishing to observe an autopsy performed on a brother, but he was no longer even sure that Carrini was the dead man's brother. He pushed through the swinging doors.

The autopsy room was a large chamber, with a high ceiling, and very old. It had obviously not been used for years; there was dust everywhere, though an attempt had recently been made to wipe it clean. The equipment was cumbersome, outdated, and rusting from years of disuse. Most of the light in the room was natural, though a heavy operating light was located on a swinging overhead bracket. The stainless steel table in the center of the room held the body, covered with a sheet.

Karin went to the wall along one side, where there were shelves and drawers. "Gloves?"

"Size eight, please."

She brought him the gloves and the gown. She helped him into the gown and tied it efficiently around his back; she held the gloves for him to slip his hands into.

He said, "You are a surgical nurse?"

"I am Dr. Garber's assistant. When he operates, I am with him."

Ross flexed his fingers inside the gloves and glanced over at Carrini, who stood in a corner of the room, near the door. Ross saw that he had apparently taken the briefcase from the fourth man and was now holding it. He considered saying something, but decided against it.

To Karin, he said, "Can you take dictation?"

"Yes."

"Then get a pad and pencil. It will save time."

She went to a cupboard and found them, then returned. Ross reached for the sheet, paused, and looked back at Carrini.

Ross drew away the sheet.

The body surprised him. It belonged to a short man, wiry, emaciated. The eyes were closed, the face frozen in a grimace of pain. Drawing the sheet farther down, he saw the abdomen. There were two neat, red, crusty punctures.

Karin said, "What will you need?"

Staring at the wounds in what he hoped was a business-like way, Ross said, "Scalpel. Number twenty blade, if you have it."

"Yes."

"And a half-dozen hemostats. Mosquito. Toothed forceps. Metzenbaum shears."

She nodded and went to get them. If he had said something wrong, she gave no indication. When she returned, she set the instruments out on a table and picked up a pad and pencil.

"You will dictate your notes, Doctor?"

"Yes," Ross said. He paused, looked at the body, and began.

"Postmortem on Stephano Carrini," he said. "An emaciated white male of—" he turned to Carrini "—how old?"

"Fifty," Carrini said.

Ross felt sure the newspaper account of the murder had described the man younger. But there was no doubt this was the body of a fifty-year-old man on the table.

"Man of fifty, hair brown, eyes—" he lifted one eyelid with his thumb "—blue, false upper dentures. No scars. Two symmetrical punctures suggestive of bullet wounds in the abdomen, lower left and upper right quadrant. Am I going too fast?"

"No, Doctor," she said.

"No other surface markings," he said, examining the body. "Except for punctures in olecranon fossa of both arms." He looked close. "Needle punctures. Was your brother an addict, Mr. Carrini?"

"For many years."

Ross checked the legs and found more punctures. He straightened and, with Karin's help, rolled the body over. The back was deep purple: dependent lividity. No markings. They returned the body to its original position.

"Scalpel, please."

He began to cut. He glanced over at Karin, but her eyes were blank and expressionless as she watched him work. He made the usual Y-shaped incision and felt it was not too clumsily done. With the organs exposed, he could see the full extent of damage. One bullet had passed upward, shattering the spleen and the left kidney behind. The other had burrowed through the liver and punctured the duodenum.

He continued to work, dictating his observations to the girl. An hour passed, and then a second. He finished with the abdominal viscera and began on the chest, cutting away the ribs with an osteo knife. He exposed the mediastinum and its contents and removed the heart.

At that point, Carrini, who had been silent, suddenly spoke. "Nurse?"

Karin looked up. "Yes?"

"Would you go out and explain the findings to my relatives? They are waiting to hear."

"You go yourself," Ross said. "She's helping me."

"I have not been able to see much from here. Besides, all that talk is meaningless to me. I am sure the girl could explain much better. Don't you, Dr. Ross?"

There was an unmistakable insistence in his voice. The girl hesitated and glanced at Ross; he saw that she was frightened.

"Go ahead," Ross said quietly. "Do as he asks."

She left the room. Carrini came forward.

"All right," Ross said, "let's get this charade over with."

Carrini had moved alongside Ross, setting the briefcase down on the edge of the table, near his brother's feet. To Ross, he said, "Now listen very carefully, Doctor. You have done an excellent job so far, and I am pleased with your work. But from now on, you are to do exactly as I say, as quickly as I can say it. No arguments: do as you're told."

He opened the briefcase. Inside was a small package the size of a man's fist. It was wrapped in a heavy, shiny black material of some kind—a bag of plastic. "Put this in the body," Carrini said. "Put it in place of the heart, and sew it up." Ross started to protest.

"No arguments!" Carrini hissed. He gave Ross the wrapped object. It was very heavy and cool, as if made of stone or metal. Ross set it inside the chest, between the lungs. It fit easily.

"Now sew," Carrini said.

"But I haven't finished—"

"Sew!"

"The girl will come back."

"My relatives will keep her occupied for at least fifteen minutes. Those were my instructions. Now sew it up."

Ross threaded a curved suture needle and began to sew. He started at the lower abdomen and worked upward in long, looping stitches. He finished in ten minutes, then stepped back from the table.

Carrini snapped the briefcase shut and walked back to his former position.

"That was very well done, Doctor," he said. "I congratulate you."

"What was it?"

"Take my advice," Carrini said. "Forget you ever saw it. It will be better if you forget."

"Heroin?"

Carrini shook his head. "Don't be a fool."

"Listen," Ross said, "there are enzymes and corrosive substances in the body. They'll destroy almost anything—"

"Forget," Carrini said, in a low voice. "Forget, forget."

The girl came back into the room. "I'm sorry to be so long," she said to Ross. "They were full of questions."

She stopped as she saw the body, sewn up.

"The postmortem is finished," Carrini announced crisply. "While you were gone, Dr. Ross concluded that nothing more of value could be learned. My brother died of multiple gunshot wounds to the abdomen. You will no doubt wish to accompany him as he writes up the report and fills out the papers."

Karin looked at Ross questioningly.

"That's right," Ross said. He pulled the sheet over the body again. They left the room. Outside, the relatives were standing about, smoking and talking quietly, very grave. Carrini said to them, "The undertakers will arrive in an hour. Wait here for them."

Carrini went with Ross and the girl to another room, where the autopsy report was briefly written up. A number of forms and papers had to be signed by Ross and countersigned by

Karin as a witness. Carrini never left them alone. And the girl continued to give Ross frightened, questioning looks.

Later, there was a moment of confusion as the undertakers arrived. Ross felt a piece of paper being slipped into his pocket. He looked over; Karin smiled slightly. No one else noticed what had happened.

Twenty minutes later, he left the sanatorium and returned by helicopter and private car to the Costa Brava.

5. BARCELONA

Back at the hotel, Carrini said, "Let me buy you a drink."

"Thanks," Ross said, "I'd rather not."

"Very sour of you, Doctor. You seem unhappy."

"Me? Unhappy? Just because you threaten to murder me, then whisk me off to perform an autopsy, and then right in the middle—"

"You have done nothing illegal," Carrini said. "You performed a straightforward autopsy, and you wrote a straightforward report. Nothing else happened." He gripped Ross's arm tightly. "Nothing. Now: a drink?"

"A drink," Ross said.

They went into the bar and sat down. Carrini relaxed, his anger vanishing as quickly as it had come. "Tell me," he said pleasantly, "what are your future plans? Will you leave Spain?"

"Well, I'm still on vacation," Ross said.

"Then you will remain here?"

"Until the conference, yes."

Carrini's body tensed slightly. "Conference?" he asked, lighting a cigarette.

"There's a conference in Barcelona in a few days. The American Society of Radiologists."

"I see," Carrini said slowly. "And you are attending?"

"Yes. I'm delivering a paper."

"I see."

"Does that surprise you?"

"Surprise me? No, indeed. I congratulate you. I had no idea you were so distinguished."

The drinks came. Carrini raised his glass. "Your health."

They drank. Carrini finished his quickly, then said, "Oh, there is one other thing. I owe you some money." He reached for his checkbook.

"You owe me nothing."

"I thought we agreed—"

"Let's just say," Ross said, "that I did it out of friendship."

Carrini smiled. "You are a fool. Take the money. You earned it."

"No."

"But I insist."

"No, thank you."

Carrini sighed. "As you wish." He stood to go. "Then it seems our business is concluded."

"I hope so," Ross said.

"So do I," Carrini said, and his voice was coldly serious.

He found her on the beach. It was late afternoon, and the sun was falling, turning the water to lapping gold. An evening breeze was blowing up; she had goose pimples.

"Where have you been? I looked everywhere for you."

"I've been to the sanatorium."

"The what?"

"The Heitzman Sanatorium. North of Barcelona."

"What for?"

He sat down on the sand. "For an autopsy," he said.

"You did it?"

He nodded.

"What happened?"

"Nothing. It was just an autopsy. Two bullet wounds. He was definitely dead."

She shivered. "Don't tell me about it," she said. "Are you all right?"

"Yes, I think so."

"You look frightened."

"Just confused, really. But I don't think there's any danger now." He stared out at the ocean and the reddened, angry sun.

"I hope not," she said. She took his hand.

"Anything I can do for you?" she asked. He looked at her, her dark hair, her tan, the outrageous pink bikini, and her goose pimples.

"Maybe," he said. "It's pretty cold out here."

She kissed his ear. "Somewhere else?"

Much later, while she was taking a shower in his room, he remembered the note. He searched through his pockets and found it, a small, carefully folded piece of paper. The words were hastily scrawled.

CALL ME BARCELONA
K BRENNER

He stared at the note and thought about the frightened girl. He thought about Carrini, and then he found himself thinking about everything, the whole business. He slipped the message back in his pocket as Angela came out of the shower, wrapped in a towel.

"And now, the latest creation. Straight from the greatest couturier collection of all. We call this one 'Thirteenth Rib.' "

She threw the towel away and pirouetted for him.

"It's the basis for the new line this year," she said. "It's supposed to appeal to men. It comes in a variety of styles to suit every occasion."

"I'll take it just as it is," he said.

"Will you?" she asked, raising an eyebrow.

"I will," he said, forgetting about the message.

❁

It was over dinner that Angela said, "Maybe we should go somewhere else for a few days."

"Like where?"

"I don't know. Anywhere. France, or Majorca, or Tangier. Even Barcelona."

He nodded. "Perhaps you're right."

"Barcelona's fun. Ever been?"

He shook his head.

"Then why don't we?"

"All right," he said. "Let's."

They left in the morning.

Barcelona: the largest city in Spain, the wealthiest, the most vibrant. Sprawling along the coast and back into the hills, by turns peaceful and raucous, elegant and tawdry, serene and violent. The port, at the end of Calle Ramblas, was crude, noisy, filled with whores, brawling sailors, day laborers. Back in the hills, near the modern university, the residential sections were fashionable and secluded.

They stayed in the center of town, in a large hotel off the Plaza Cataluna, with a room with a balcony overlooking the fountains.

Angela said she wanted to shop, but Ross refused to accompany her, saying he hated to shop with women; it was a personal thing, no offense intended.

"And what are you going to do while you're alone?"

He shrugged. "Walk around. See the sights."

"Meet me back here in two hours? For lunch?"

"Of course."

"Promise?"

"Yes," he laughed.

When she was gone, he hunted through the telephone

directory for Karin Brenner's name. He found it, at an address in the north of town.

He called. The phone rang six times, and then a cautious voice answered.

"Yes?"

"Miss Brenner?"

"Who is calling?"

"Dr. Ross."

"Oh," she said, with a little sob. "Oh, I'm so frightened, Doctor."

"Why?"

"I must talk to you." Her voice was quavering, on the edge of hysteria.

"What's the matter?"

"Oh, I'm so frightened." A little gasp. "I know what has happened."

"What?"

"The thing you put in the body. I know what it is."

"How do you know about that?" Ross was frowning.

"Before, I was listening to the cousins. It was an accident; they did not know I was near. I heard them argue. About X-rays. What would happen if the body was X-rayed. I heard everything. I must talk to you."

"All right. When?"

"Immediately," she said. "I have just come from the library, and I am beginning to understand."

"Understand what?"

"Come," she said. "We will talk."

He hung up and took a cab to her apartment. It turned out to be a huge, modern high-rise in the northern suburbs. Her apartment was on the tenth floor. He took the elevator up and knocked on the door.

No answer.

He knocked again and waited.

No answer.

"Karin? Are you there?"

He tried the knob. The door was unlocked. He went in. The living room was empty, but very tidy and neat, with unmistakable feminine touches. There were bright pillows on the couch, a rack of fashion magazines, mostly French.

"Karin?"

He went into the next room, a small bedroom with barely room for a single bed. The bed was unmade and empty, the rumpled sheets contrasting oddly with the neatness of the living room.

Behind him, the door slammed. He felt a cold, sharp point against the base of his neck.

"Don't move."

He did not. A moment later, the point was removed. He heard sobbing and turned around. It was Karin. She was leaning against the door, crying. The knife had dropped to the floor.

"I'm sorry," she said. "So sorry. But I was afraid..."

"It's all right now," he said, comforting her. He took her back to the living room, made her sit on the couch, and poured her a brandy. Then he locked the front door. When she had sipped the brandy and wiped her eyes, she seemed better.

"You all right?"

"Yes, I think so."

"Can I get you something else? Coffee? Tea?"

She nodded, "Tea, thank you." Ross went into the kitchen to make it. In the kitchen, he found a half-finished cup of coffee next to the stove. Nearby was an ashtray with several stubbed-out cigarettes. And five books in a careful stack.

They were old books, dusty: library books, from the University of Barcelona. The titles struck him as odd.

Prescott: *The Conquest of Mexico.* He opened the book; a marker had been placed in the section concerning "The Marriage of Cortez."

He looked at the others.

Henriques: *Aztec Civilization.*

Marston-Thomas: *The Life of Cortes.*

Quirnal: *Artifacts des Aztecs.*

And finally, a thick book in Spanish of genealogies. There were two markers here: one for a page describing the house of Arellano, the noble family of Navarre; the other, the House of Bejar. Neither name meant anything to Ross.

He looked at the library cards.

The books had all been checked out the day before.

Odd.

He put the kettle on to boil and returned to the living room. She was smoking a cigarette tensely.

"Now then," he said. "What's this all about?"

"I am afraid," she said softly. "Because I know everything. I overheard the men talking. Do you know a man they call the professor?"

"The professor? What's his real name?"

She shrugged. "They just called him the professor."

"No," Ross said, thinking. "Never heard of him."

"And the count?"

He shook his head again. "No."

"They talked about these two men," Karin said. "The professor and the count. They made jokes about the shipment. They said the shipment would go to Portugal. And they laughed: *The shipment would go to Portugal.* And then something about America. Do you understand this?"

"No," Ross admitted. "It means nothing to me at all. What else did they say?"

"The object," she said. "They talked about the object you put in the body. Can you describe it for me?"

"Not really. It was about the size of your hand, and very heavy, and square—"

"Square? Are you sure?"

"Well, at least it was in a square box of some kind."

"You are certain of this?"

"Yes. But why? What was it? And what are all those books in the kitchen about Mexico?"

"They are about Cortez," she corrected.

"Cortez?"

"He is the key to everything."

"Cortez?"

She nodded.

At that moment, the doorbell rang, a low, musical chime. They both froze. Karin looked at Ross questioningly; he shook his head. The doorbell rang again, and then a heavy hand knocked on the door.

A muffled voice said, "Karin? You there?"

Neither of them moved. They heard a hand twist the doorknob, but the door was locked.

At that moment, the boiling water began a shrill whistle. Ross looked up in horror; Karin leaped up and knocked over an ashtray, which fell to the floor with a thump.

The knocking at the door began again.

"I must answer it," Karin whispered. "Go to the kitchen."

Aloud, she called, "Just a minute, please."

She waited until Ross had gone to the kitchen and turned off the water; then she answered the door. Ross listened, ears straining, but he could hear only low voices. There seemed to be a whispered argument of some kind. Then there was a rustling, or a scuffling.

And then the door slammed shut.

He hesitated in the kitchen, waiting for her to come back to him. When she did not, he looked cautiously out into the living room.

Karin lay on the floor, not moving. Her face was blue-black, and there was an angry red ring around her neck. He bent over her quickly, feeling for a pulse. The pulse was there, but very slow. He saw that she was breathing. He shook her gently.

"Karin. Karin."

She did not respond. He shook her harder, but there was still no response.

Then he heard sirens, at first in the distance, but coming closer. Somehow he knew the sirens were coming to Karin's apartment. He got up and opened the door, peering out into the hallway. No one there. He made a dash for the elevators, punched the down button, and waited; the lights overhead showed the elevators were both on the ground floor. As he watched, he saw that they both began to ascend.

He ran to the service stairs. As he opened the door leading down, he heard the tramp of boots coming up.

Trapped.

Someone had set it up, set it up very neatly and carefully. And he had fallen into it.

He returned to the hallway and looked up and down desperately. All the doors were shut, except for one, which was slightly ajar. From the inside, he heard Latin music.

He glanced at the elevator lights. The elevators were already to the eighth floor. The police were closing in.

He had no choice. He knocked on the door that was ajar and pushed it open.

"Excuse me," he said as he entered the room and closed the door behind him, "But I am afraid I—"

He stopped.

And stared, as anyone might, when faced with a beautiful girl, standing in the middle of her apartment at midday, wearing a very sheer nightgown, and beneath that, nothing at all.

"Lover!" she cried, and flung her arms around him.

6. SERVICES RENDERED

He had no objection, really. She was very warm and soft and blonde and cuddly, and the warmth was catching. She had nice soft lips, and she held him tightly, dragging him back to the couch. They fell, and the springs creaked loudly.

He finally managed to pull back, "But we hardly know each other," he said.

"Kiss me, kiss me," she sighed.

She pulled him down on her, and they kissed again.

"Allow me to introduce—"

"Later baby, later," she said.

They kissed more, and while they were kissing, she wriggled against him and messed his hair and did various other little things which, in the back of his mind, he appreciated.

It was then that the police knocked on the door and entered immediately afterward. They looked up from the couch at the man in the uniform, who blushed deeply and excused himself in quick Spanish. The door slammed shut again.

The girl sat up and pushed Ross away. She put on a quilted housejacket, lit a cigarette, and said, "That will be two hundred dollars, please."

"What?"

"Two hundred dollars, lover."

"What for?"

"Services rendered," she said.

"I don't under—"

"If it seems excessive," she said, "I can always scream.

The police will be back in seconds. And I will explain how you burst into my apartment, running from them, and—"

"Two hundred dollars," he said, reaching for his wallet. He counted out the bills and set them on the coffee table.

As the girl scooped them up, she said, "Do you want it?"

"Want what?"

"Cost you another two hundred, you know." She smiled slightly. "Inflation. The rising spiral of wages and prices. Supply and demand. You know?"

"Not really," he said. He was puzzled by her. She had a blonde, American wholesomeness and an American accent. "What's your name?"

"Suzy," she said. "Gordon. I am employed by the American consul in Barcelona."

"Oh?"

"In a private capacity."

"Oh?"

"In a very private capacity. You must know about the public sector and the private sector. All that stuff. Well, there's the public parts and the private parts, too."

"Oh?"

"And besides, he is a very dear man."

"Oh?"

"He is a perfect example of what I call the gross national product."

"Oh."

"But he's rich, you see. That helps."

"Oh?"

"However, I also do other kinds of work. Listen, the economics of this business are fascinating. I pay income tax, you know. I'm a law-abiding public servant."

"I see."

"Now then," she said, "you're the doctor, right?"

"Right."

"Okay." She went to a corner of the room and came back with a paper bag. "I'm authorized to negotiate with you."

"You are?"

"Sure. There's no point in acting surprised, lover. I know you're smarter than you act. At least, I hope you are. What are you asking?"

"For what?"

"For everything you know. I'm authorized to negotiate."

"I don't understand."

"*Information*, baby," she said, stubbing out her cigarette. "That's what we want."

"We?"

"Of course. Now what are you asking?"

"I'm not asking anything."

"Play it as cagey as you want. I'll give you five thousand dollars."

He watched as she reached into the paper bag and brought out five stacks of bills. Each was bound with a paper strip on which was marked "$1000."

She stepped back from the table. "Well?"

"What can I say?"

"Say where the shipment is."

"The shipment?"

She winced, reached into the bag, and brought out five more bundles of bills.

"The *body*, baby," she said. "Say where it is."

"What body?"

"Listen, sweetmeat, this is serious business. You're dealing with an obsession, you know? The guy really *cares*. You want more? Fifteen thousand?"

"No."

"Why not? Because you can't be bought?"

"Because I don't know anything," Ross said.

"Bullshit," she said.

Ross stood. "I'm sorry we have to part this way."

She scooped up the money and dropped it into the paper bag. "You're making a mistake."

"But I'll always remember you fondly."

"You could get killed."

"Even on my deathbed, I will remember little Suzy—"

"I'm not so little."

"—and her stacks of money."

She smiled and patted his cheek. "You're a love," she said. "Just be careful, huh? I'd hate to see you get killed."

"So would I."

"And the chances are you will get killed."

"I'm beginning to suspect you're right."

"I usually am," Suzy said. "It's because you won't play the game."

"I'd play," Ross said, "if I only knew the rules."

"But you see," Suzy said, "that's the way the game is. Nobody knows the rules."

"Not much of a game."

"Well, it depends."

As he was leaving, she said. "By the way, better wipe that lipstick off your face before you go. You look like you've been through a pretty wild time."

"I have," Ross said, and closed the door behind him.

7. THE MARRIAGE OF CORTEZ

Angela was in the hotel room, her shoes kicked off, lying on the bed and drinking a Scotch.

"You're late," she said.

"I know," he said. "I got held up."

"Oh?"

"Yes," he said. He took her drink and swallowed it in a long gulp.

"Hey!"

"Sorry. I was thirsty."

She went to the phone. "I'll call for more. Maybe they'll send up a better-looking bellboy. The last one was ugly. Lucky for you."

"No," Ross said, putting the phone down. "We're going out now."

"Lunch?"

"No. Bookstore."

"Bookstore? What for?"

"I have to do a little research."

The concierge directed them to a large, cosmopolitan shop in the center of town.

"What kind of book do you want?" Angela said.

"A book about Mexico."

"Why Mexico?"

"Curiosity."

He asked a salesman for a copy in English of Prescott's *The Conquest of Mexico*. The salesman was a haughty Spaniard in very tight pants.

"We have only the abridged version," he said.

"I'll take it."

It turned out to be a cheap, dusty copy with small print, yellowing pages, and a twenty-dollar price tag. Ross paid it, and they went out and caught a taxi.

"You seem awfully curious," Angela said. "For twenty dollars."

"I am."

"Is this a sudden urge? Or do you often get these fits of academic interest?"

Ross didn't answer. He directed the cab driver to a restaurant, then sat back. He thumbed through the index.

"Cortez, Cortez…here we are. Marriage of Cortez."

Angela frowned. "Marriage of Cortez?"

"That's right."

He turned to the correct page, and squinted to read the small print. It was a very short section, no more than three paragraphs.

"I don't get it," he said when he finished. He closed the book.

Angela waited.

"All it says is that when Cortez returned from Mexico, he wanted to be governor of the new country, but that Charles V denied his request. Charles wanted him to win more battles for him. Cortez stayed in Spain for a while and courted Dona Juana de Zuniga, who was very beautiful."

"Naturally."

"Naturally. He married her."

"Naturally."

"Yes. And it says here—" he opened the book again, "that she was daughter of the second count of Aguilar, and niece of the duke of Bejar, and was of the House of Arellano, of the royal lineage of Navarre."

He stopped. Those were the names Karin had been looking up in the genealogy books. Those same names.

Angela said, "Something wrong?"

"No, no. Just thinking."

"Relatives of yours?"

Ross laughed. "Hardly," he said.

Angela sighed. "Well, that's all fine for Cortez, but why did you want to know so badly?"

"Damned if I know," Ross said. He scratched his head. "Wait a minute. This book is abridged. Maybe there's something else, in the full-length version."

"Something else?"

"Yes."

"Like what?"

"I don't know," Ross admitted.

The taxi pulled up at the restaurant.

"So much for research," Ross said.

"I'm starved," Angela said.

Over lunch, Angela said, "What will we do tomorrow?"

"Well, there's something I haven't told you."

She frowned. "Yes?"

"I have a meeting."

"Tomorrow?"

"Yes."

"More about this autopsy business?"

He shook his head. "This is respectable. The American Society of Radiologists."

"You're kidding," she said.

"I'm registering," he said.

"I'm stuck with an establishment creep," she said.

"That's right," he said.

"Zero cool," she said, "and no points for me."

"Well, perhaps one or two," he said.

"Yes," she said. "Come to think of it."

Part II

"The diagnostic skills of the radiologist are significant, but limited."
— HAROLD ELLISON, M.D.

PROLOGUE

The hearse drove through the moonless night, churning a dark plume of dust behind it. It passed through desolate, barren country, a land of sand and naked rock.

In the driver's seat, the Arab said, "Where is it?" The man next to him squinted, peering forward in the light of the headlamps. "Just ahead."

The Arab glanced at the rearview mirror. No one was following them. It was midnight and everyone, even the trucks, were off the road.

"We turn soon?"

"Immediately, See the shack there? Turn left." The Arab slowed the hearse and made the turn as they came to it. The car bounced off the asphalt highway onto a dirt road. They drove in silence for several minutes, and then the man said, "Look there."

An American station wagon was parked off to one side of the road. "Pull over."

The Arab pulled over. They got out of the hearse and walked in the cool night air to the station wagon. The keys were where they were supposed to be, beneath the seat.

They returned to the hearse and opened the rear doors. The coffin, made of simple pine, was pulled out and carried by them to the station wagon. They slipped it into the back and covered it with a blanket.

"Well," the Arab said, wiping his hands on his trousers, "that's done."

"Not quite. We must take care of the car."

"*Back at the main road?*"

"*Yes. It will appear more natural.*"

The Arab got behind the wheel of the hearse and drove it back to the highway. The other man followed in the station wagon. It was several minutes before they reached the asphalt. The Arab then turned left and drove down the road for several miles. The station wagon followed, and then blinked its high-beam lights.

Abruptly, the Arab drove the hearse off the road into a gully. He got out, and the man parked the station wagon and came forward with the gun.

"*You do it,*" *the man said.*

Carefully, the Arab took the gun and shot at the hearse. He shattered the front windshield and the side window on the driver's side, leaving a series of sharp, round holes in the glass. When he was satisfied, he stepped back and waited for the other man to sprinkle gasoline all over the inside of the car.

"*You know,*" *the Arab said, watching as the gas soaked the seats,* "*I wonder about this.*"

"*Wonder? Why?*"

"*Remember Edouardo? Remember what happened to him when he tried to—*"

"*Edouardo. Edouardo was a fool.*"

"*Yes, but the way he died…*"

"*It does not matter, how you die.*"

"*But those cuts. What could have done it?*"

"*It does not matter,*" *the other man insisted. He nodded to the Arab.* "*Light the car.*"

The Arab struck a match, stepped back, and threw it into the hearse. Immediately, the gasoline caught; with a roar, the entire car burst into flames.

"Come on," the other man said. "The gas tank will explode soon."

They ran back to the station wagon, started it, and drove back toward the dirt road. They had not gone more than a hundred yards when the gasoline tank of the hearse blew with a sound like a heavy growl, and a rush of hot air.

"There won't be anything left," the Arab said, looking back.

"That's the idea," the other man said, and smiled slightly.

8. A SHOT IN THE ARM

The notices Ross had received stated that registration was from nine to twelve in the Excelsior Hotel lobby. At nine thirty, they finished breakfast, and he walked with Angela up the street to the hotel, which was only a few blocks away.

It was a warm, sunny day. Ross felt relaxed and good, a kind of lazy, easygoing feeling.

A car pulled up, and two men jumped out. They grabbed Ross. One had a gun.

Angela began to scream, very loudly. She shouted for the police, and one man struck her across the mouth while the other shoved Ross into the car. He struggled silently with the man but he was losing, pushed steadily toward the car. Inside the open door, he could see two other men waiting.

Then it all went black.

Cold water. He shook his head, felt dampness. Nausea. He was sick on a wooden floor. More cold water.

"Come on. Get up." A harsh, American voice.

He was sick again. Dizzy, painful. His head throbbed.

"Get up, get up."

Strong arms lifted him, dragged him, dropped him into a chair. He shook his head to clear it, to stop the terrible pain.

"You'll be all right. Open your eyes."

He did. The room was small. Three men. It began to spin. He smelled his vomit and felt sick again. He closed his eyes.

"Come on, mister. We haven't got all day."

He took a deep breath, fighting the nausea and the dizziness. For a moment, he thought he would pass out, but then the feeling left him. He opened his eyes again. The room was steady. The three men were still there, and he recognized their faces—they were the relatives who had come to his room that first day, in Tossa del Mar. The relatives who had been at the sanatorium.

"That's better," one said. He turned to another man. "Search him."

Ross was quickly frisked. They found nothing except the copy of the book, which he had stuck in his pocket before setting out that morning. He looked around the room. It could have been anywhere—small, wooden walls, wooden floor. No windows except a small one, high near the ceiling. No furniture, except the chair in which he sat. There was a telephone, ancient and battered, hanging on one wall.

The book was handed over to the first man. He was pale, thin, mean-looking. Ross remembered him. He had been silent, impassive, at the earlier meetings.

"Where's Carrini?" Ross said.

"Busy," the man said. "As you can imagine."

"I can?"

The thin man slapped him, casually but very hard. "Now then, mister. Tell us, and tell us quickly."

"Tell you what? Where am I?"

He was slapped again. His cheek stung, and his head rocked with the blow.

"Tell us," the man said quietly, "where the body is."

"The body?"

"Don't be stubborn, mister. We haven't got all day."

"You mean this is a part-time job?"

For that, he received another slap and a punch in the stomach.

"Gee," he said, "and you were so polite before. People are funny."

Someone hit him again, knocking him to the floor. His head began to spin once more, and he vomited.

"Maybe we should take it easy," a voice said. "He's no good to us—"

"He knows. I'm sure he knows."

Ross looked back up and wiped his chin. "I don't know anything."

"Then what are you doing with this?" the thin man demanded. He held up the book.

"I bought it yesterday."

"So you know, eh?"

"No."

"You wouldn't buy this book if you didn't."

"I don't. I was trying to find out. The book didn't help."

"The hell. You'd better—"

Silence. A sudden, dead silence in the room. Ross looked behind him and saw Carrini standing just inside the door.

"Well," Carrini said. "Well, well. Is this what we have come to?"

"Boss," the thin man said, "he's being stubborn, and—"

"And you decided to work him over."

"It was the only way—"

"It wasn't," Carrini said quietly. "And it leaves marks. Did you ever think of that? This man is a doctor, and he's attending a conference here. We can't have him walking around with bruises. That wouldn't do at all."

The thin man looked confused.

"Sit down, Rico," Carrini said. "We will talk about you later."

He stepped forward to Ross. "I am sorry to inconvenience you, Doctor."

"That's all right," Ross said. "I don't get enough exercise, anyway. Nothing like a beating to keep a man in shape, eh?"

Carrini sighed. "I must apologize for these men. They mean well—"

"I noticed."

"—but they lack finesse. As you may have gathered, the reason for bringing you here is to ask you some questions."

"I've been trying to tell them I don't know anything."

Carrini nodded reasonably. "That's quite possible."

He reached into his pocket and brought out a syringe and ampul. He set them on the table.

"Would you roll up your sleeve, please?"

"What is that?"

"Sodium amytal solution. I trust you understand."

"Listen, I don't—"

"I am afraid," Carrini said, "that we must insist."

Strong hands gripped him. He felt himself held tightly; his sleeve was rolled up and a tourniquet placed on his arm. There was a cool alcohol swab, and then a prick of a needle.

"Good," Carrini said, stepping back. The tourniquet was released.

"Now, Doctor. Please count backward for us. From one hundred."

"Go to hell," Ross said.

Carrini smiled. Ross waited for the drug to take effect, but nothing was happening. The four men were staring at him, but nothing was happening.

Carrini sniffed the air. "What's that smell?"

One of the others smiled sheepishly. "Aftershave."

"It smells terrible."

"It was free," another man said. "They gave it away."

"Gave it away? Where?"

"Free samples. In the hotel. This girl was handing them out."

"What kind of girl?"

A shrug. "Some blonde."

Carrini said, "Well, don't wear it again. It stinks to high heaven." He turned to Ross. "Will you count now?"

"Go to hell," Ross said. He could see perfectly well. There was no blurring, no fuzziness, no slowness. Carrini was there, and he could see him well. Very well.

"What?"

"Go to hell."

Carrini leaned close. "I can't hear you."

"I said…"

Ross stopped. He couldn't remember. It was funny, but he just couldn't remember what he had meant to say. Very funny how you wanted to say something and you knew you wanted to say something but you couldn't remember…

"What?"

Ross shook his head. He did not want to talk. He was becoming sleepy. Very, very sleepy. He felt his body sag and go heavy. It was good to close his eyes, to shut away the bright light. Inside his head, it was peaceful and serene. Everything was gentle.

When Carrini spoke again, his voice was resonant, deep and thoughtful, and gentle and serene.

"The body," Carrini said, "has been stolen…"

Inside his head, Ross heard the words echo: *stolen, stolen, stolen…*

"Where is it being taken…"

Where, where, where, where…

"Answer me…"

Answer, answer, answer…

The words were colored red. Floating through the air, red-colored words, vibrant and beautiful.

"Answer me…"

He took a deep breath, seeing the air rush into his lungs, seeing his blood turn red with oxygen, feeling himself grow strong to speak, and he said:

"Portugal…"

"Where?"

"Port-u-gal…"

"How do you know?"

"She."

She had told him. She had told him all about it, she had overheard everything, and she had told him.

"Who?"

"The girl…Karin…"

"She is wrong," Carrini said. "Tell us where."

"Portugal…"

And then it became very dark. He could see nothing and hear nothing. But he knew questions were coming, because his ears tingled, and he knew he was answering, because his jaw was vibrating and moving. But he could not hear the questions, and he could not hear the answers. It was all too dark to hear.

In his half-sleep, he recognized that they did not believe him. They were unhappy with his answers, and this made him sad, because he wanted them to believe him, to realize that he was telling them and was doing his best.

And still later, there were screams, and screeches, and a leathery slapping sound, and a strong hot wind. But it might have been a dream. It all might have been a dream.

9. A LITTLE BIT TIRED

He awoke like a man suffocating beneath a hundred very heavy blankets. He struggled, pushing them aside one by one, rising slowly to the surface and to cool air. He struggled for a long time, and then he felt a mild breeze and lay back, gasping for breath, and his eyes closed.

He rested that way for a long time. How long, he did not know, but then he began to smell a strange, sick-sweet odor. He opened his eyes and found himself staring at the ceiling.

The ceiling was whitewashed, with a diagonal crack running through the plaster. But that was not what caught his eye. What he saw were the red streaks: they were everywhere, in a long, haphazard pattern. Dark red and ugly looking. Like welts on a ceiling.

Odd.

He glanced over at the wall and saw more streaks. A mad painter, gone berserk, flinging his brush wildly around the room—that was the way it looked. Except that this was not paint.

He sat up and looked around him. For a moment, he could not believe it; it was like an illusion, an elaborately posed and grisly still life.

In one corner, Carrini. His body slashed and torn, his clothes shredded, his neck cut through, his face ripped almost beyond recognition. He lay propped against the wall, in a spreading pool of his own blood.

In other parts of the room, the other three men. Each had died the same violent death. One man had his stomach torn open; another, his arms and shoulders; the third had deep slashes in the skull which had opened to expose white bone. And there was blood everywhere.

Ross felt sick and retched dryly; he had a wave of dizziness and closed his eyes until the world stopped spinning. When he opened them again, the men were still there. The men, and the walls, and the blood. He could not imagine who had done such a thing. He could not imagine how or when it had happened. Apparently, he had slept through it all.

And he was untouched. Strange, that the others should be killed but he permitted to live.

He explored his body, feeling for broken bones, but he was apparently all right. He felt weak and had a splitting headache, but that was all. After a few minutes, he stood, leaning on the chair.

More dizziness. He waited, and it passed. He walked out of the room and found himself in a warehouse. It was a long, giant room, filled with cardboard boxes, which apparently contained furniture for export to Italy. He walked to the far end of the warehouse and found another door, which led out to the street.

He walked until he saw a cab. It was eleven o'clock; only an hour and a half had passed since the men had picked him up and pushed him into the car. It seemed like years. He got into the cab and returned to his hotel. He would have to clean himself up before he registered. And he wanted to see Angela.

In the hotel, the concierge rushed up to him. "Are you all right, sir?"

Ross was feeling better. Weak, but better. "Yes."

"Was it an accident?"

"What?"

The concierge gestured vaguely to his clothes. "An accident?"

"Yes," Ross said. "I fell, and a car…"

"You wish a doctor?"

"I think so," he said touching his forehead. "I may need X-rays."

"If you go to your room, I will call the doctor. He is very good. Trained in New York," the concierge said.

Ross went to his room.

"Well howdy."

Ross closed the door behind him. The cowboy, still dressed in his leather and fringes, lay casually on the bed.

"Hello," Ross said.

He was not surprised to see him. Nothing would have surprised him. Not now.

"You look a tad beat-up, boy," the cowboy said.

"I'm a little bit tired," Ross said.

"Get into a scrape?"

"You might say so." He dropped into a chair. "Where's Angela?"

"Is that your girl?"

"Yes."

"I asked her to leave for a while, so's we could be alone." The cowboy smiled. "Mighty fine piece of woman, if I say so myself. Mighty fine."

"I'm glad you like her."

"Oh, I do, I do. I never exaggerate, where women are concerned."

"That's good," Ross said. He sighed. "And what are you and I going to do, now that we're alone?"

"Just talk."

"You don't want to beat me up?"

"Heck no, son."

"It's the thing to do," Ross said. "Everyone's trying it."

"Heck no, I just want a peaceable chat."

Ross sighed. "Chat away. Going to introduce yourself first?"

"You can call me Tex."

"You're joking," Ross said.

"Nope. Tex. Everybody does. Natural enough: that's my name."

Tex gave a laugh, a big, booming, hearty laugh.

"You can call me Doc," Ross said.

"I like that," Tex said, nodding seriously.

"Okay, Tex. What's on your mind? I suppose you're playing the game, too?"

"What game's that?"

"Body, body, who's got the body," Ross said.

Tex smiled. "You're a sharpie, boy. I knew it from the start." He paused. "That why you were beat up?"

"Right."

"I told you to be careful."

"I was doing my best," Ross said.

"Oh, don't take it to heart. I'm sure those fellas didn't mean anything personal."

"I'm sure," Ross said. "Were they friends of yours?"

"Hell no," Tex said.

There was a short silence. Tex stared at Ross for a moment, then said, "What finally happened to them?"

"Them?"

"The fellas who beat you up."

"Why do you ask?"

"Because you're hardly scratched. Just a bruise or two."

"So?"

"So I'm wondering why you got blood caked an inch thick on your shoes."

"It's their blood," Ross said.

"Their blood?"

"I killed them," Ross said. "All twelve of them."

"Now son, you're pulling my leg."

Ross smiled slightly. "Am I?"

A knock on the door. The doctor arrived. Tex sat patiently on the bed and waited while the doctor examined Ross and pronounced him battered but fit. Ross was advised to stay in bed for a few days and to have someone around in case he lost consciousness. There was always the chance of a subdural hematoma. Ross nodded, knowing that he would never have a chance to stay in bed.

When the doctor left, Tex said, "Probably you ought to take a shower and change."

Ross glanced at his watch. It was past eleven thirty. He had to register. "No time," he said.

"Sure there's time," Tex said.

"What makes you so sure?"

He shrugged. "Plane doesn't leave for another hour."

"What plane?"

"Better take your shower," Tex said. "We can talk later."

"I'm not going on any plane."

"Sure you are," Tex said.

"Why?"

"Cause I'm bigger than you," Tex said, with an easy grin. "Now don't make trouble. Just take a shower and change your clothes so you'll look respectable."

"Where am I going?"

"Paris," Tex said. "Now git."

10. PARIS

The plane lifted off the runway with jets screaming and headed northwest over dry, mountainous terrain.

"There's going to be trouble," Ross said. "I was supposed to register for the conference. When I don't—"

"No trouble," Tex said. "You've canceled out."

"I have?"

"Yesterday," Tex said, "to be exact."

"Says who?"

"Says me. I made the telephone call. Can't really attend a conference when you're laid up in your room with the trots, can you? Hell, any bunch of doctors understands that."

Ross frowned. "I should have said something to Angela before I left."

"Don't fret. You'll be back before she misses you."

"I will?"

"Sure. This is just a little meeting. No problem. A peaceable little meeting."

Ross said, "She's all right, isn't she?"

"The girl?"

Ross nodded.

"More than all right. She's a fine hunk of girl. Best I've seen in many a moon." Tex laughed. "How about a drink?"

"Ugh," Ross said. He felt suddenly queasy.

"Sorry," Tex said. "I forgot."

Tex stared out the window. "Love this country," he said. "Reminds me of home."

"Where's home?"

"Texas, of course."

"Never been," Ross said.

"You ought to go, sometime," Tex said. "Fine place."

Ross sighed. "I'll go, first chance."

"Do that," Tex said.

Ross closed his eyes and discovered that he was very tired, with the dragging fatigue of a man confused. The gentle motion of the plane was soothing. He looked out the window at the soft patterns of the clouds, fluffed like pillows, and he drifted off to sleep.

It was raining in Paris when they arrived, a light, warm, summer drizzle from low clouds which obscured the Eiffel Tower. Tex gave directions in surprisingly good French to the taxi driver.

"Sorry to drag you all this way," Tex said to Ross. "You look real pooped."

"Nothing like a beating," Ross said, "to poop you."

"God's truth," Tex said. "But I had to bring you, you know. I had to."

"Why?"

"He's very particular about meeting people face to face. It's a thing with him. Got to meet them face to face. You wouldn't think so, him being the way he is, but that's how it is."

"Who?"

"You."

"No. Who am I meeting?"

"Whom," Tex said absently. He sighed. "The professor."

"The professor," Ross repeated, nodding dumbly. "And who is the professor?"

"You'll see."

The taxi drew up before a large mansion, heavy, imposing, solidly constructed. It was set back from the road and partially concealed by gardens which once were elegantly formal but now had grown thick and tangled from neglect. The mansion itself was also in disrepair; it needed paint for the shutters, which were flaking and falling from their hinges. Several windows had been broken but had not been replaced; they were patched with cardboard and newspaper.

They got out of the taxi, walked through the gates and up the steps to the massive door. There was a knocker in the shape of a snarling dog's head.

"The professor lives here?" Ross said.

"He does," Tex said. He rapped loudly with the brass head.

Immediately, it was opened by an irritable woman in a maid's uniform. She led them up broad, creaking stairs to the second floor and into a small room. There was a desk, and twelve telephones arranged on shelves, and a short man with curly blond hair and large, brooding, feminine eyes.

"Mr. Jackman," Tex said. "The professor's secretary." Mr. Jackman stood and came scurrying forward, hand extended.

"Dr. Ross, I presume. How absolutely *marvelous* to meet you. I've heard *so* much about you."

He shook Ross's hand quickly, as if he were shaking out a match.

"The professor will be *most* glad to see you," Jackman said. He turned to Tex. "He's been in such a state all day. Absolutely *impossible*."

Jackman took Ross by the elbow and steered him toward the door. "But now that you're here, things will be delightful. You'll like the professor; he's such a dear. You'll enjoy talking to him."

He started to open the door for Ross, then stopped.

"I assure you there will be no problem. Just relax—be yourself, you know…and of course, don't lie. The professor *hates* that."

Ross nodded.

"Really. Bad for his heart. He gets positively apoplectic. Do bear that in mind." The door was opened. Ross was pushed through. The door was closed. Ross found himself in a long, low room carpeted in blue. It was filled with chest-high tables, slanted, like architects' drawing boards. Along one wall was a shelf of books; otherwise, the room was empty, except for a solitary figure working over one table at the far end of the room. The man was fat and chalky pale; he wore a blue serge suit and a tie which, Ross noticed, had a naked woman painted on it.

"Well, well," said the man, looking up at Ross. "Well, well."

He looked down at his papers on the drawing board, sighed, and pushed them aside.

"How nice of you to come," he said. "I take it you're Ross."

"Yes."

"You're younger than I expected. I anticipated that you would be thirty-four, five-feet eleven-inches tall, and weigh one hundred seventy-four pounds. You don't."

"No," Ross said.

"Hmmm," the professor said. He walked to another board and shuffled among the papers. "I have the figures here someplace. Know Gödel?"

"Who?"

"Kurt Gödel. Meddlesome fool. His theorem continues to plague me."

"What?"

"Gödel's Theorem," the professor said, sternly. "That damned nuisance."

Ross said nothing.

"Theorem states that certain proofs cannot be proved. Of course, he's right. That's the problem."

"I see."

He continued to search among the papers, then brought one up. "Ah, here we are. It was simple: regression and probability. How old are you?"

"Twenty-six."

"My, my. And your height?"

"Six feet."

"Weight?"

"One eighty."

"My, my. Quite unexpected." He picked up a slide rule, worked it in frowning silence, then wrote down some figures. "What do you know? The odds against your being that height, age, and weight are 14,724 to one."

"Sorry," Ross said.

The professor shrugged. "These things happen. It's all accounted for in the equations. Confidence limits are quite broad. Frustrating. One likes to pinpoint things better, but it isn't always possible. And then there's the random factor."

"The random factor?"

"Probability of indeterminate events. What we call single event prediction. At least, what I call single event prediction— I invented it. Very low state of understanding, right now, unless you go to tenth-order equations."

"I see."

"But that's neither here nor there. We all have our little problems."

"Yes."

The professor fingered the knot of his tie, making the naked girl move. He sighed.

"Come and sit down. I'll tell you what this is all about."

"I'd appreciate that."

"I'm sure. I'm sure."

They went to the back of the room, past the rows of tables. Ross looked at the tables briefly as he passed: the papers were scattered, disorganized, covered with numbers and symbols.

At the end, there were two chairs and a table. On the table was a map of Spain.

They sat down.

"Now then," the professor said, adjusting his bulk with a little shiver. "Let me tell you about our work. We are incorporated, you see. United Synthesis, Inc."

"And what do you do?"

"We synthesize and predict. Mathematically, of course."

"Of course."

"When the occasion demands it, we also freelance. But in this particular instance, we have been retained by a client."

"Who is that?"

"Tex, of course."

"Tex?" Ross said.

"Yes," the professor said. "Tex is a wealthy man, and he has a vested interest in the, uh, object of all this. He is our client: does that surprise you?"

"Nothing surprises me," Ross said.

"Very wise," the professor said. "You see, Tex came to us some weeks ago with an interesting problem which we solved, if I may say so, with characteristic brilliance. As usual, we synthesized—a combination of the topological methods used by Euler on the seven bridges of Königsberg and the three-body problem dealt with so brilliantly by Szebehely. It worked out quite nicely."

"Did it."

"Yes. It gave us a generalized solution, of course. The specifics only began to fall into place much later."

Ross nodded.

"I can see I've lost you," the professor said. "Not surprised. Let me explain it simply: our problem is one of time and space. There are three elements involved, three groups. The situation is analogous—roughly speaking—to the so-called three-body problem of space navigation, where one must define a position in terms of, say, the earth, the moon, and a rocket. In our case, we are dealing with groups of individuals, and not inanimate objects, but the mathematics remains similar."

"Did you say *three* groups?"

"Yes. There may be more. We discussed that very question earlier in the day. The possibility of as many as five groups cannot be discounted. But at present, it is unlikely. Occam's razor."

"I see," Ross said.

"Well then, the next step in the problem is topological. Topology, as you doubtless know, is the mathematics of shapes. For example, topologists can show that a doughnut and a coffee cup are essentially the same. Both genus one. You can bend a doughnut into the shape of a coffee cup, that sort of thing. But it can get more complicated."

"Yes?"

"Indeed. Möbius strips, and Klein bottles, solids with only one surface. That sort of thing. Very tricky."

"A solid with only one surface?"

The professor shrugged. "Why not?"

Ross nodded. Why not?

"However, we don't deal with such abstruse matters. We are working with network theory, started by Euler almost two hundred years ago with the Königsberg bridges. There was a city with a river which divided the land into thirds. There was also an island in the river. The problem was whether you could cross all the bridges, and never recross any."

"And what happened?"

"Euler proved, mathematically, that it was impossible."

"I'm relieved."

"Yes. Particularly when such thinking is applied to this." He tapped the map of Spain. "This is our problem—the road system of Spain. Quite a different order from seven little bridges. But we've managed."

"Perhaps you'd better begin from the beginning."

"Well," the professor said, "the beginning was quite simple. Tex came to us. He'd heard about the discovery, and he wanted an analysis."

"The discovery?"

"Yes. In Naples. That was where they found it, you know."

"Actually, I didn't," Ross said.

"Tex told us who had it and asked us to determine what they would do with it. We worked on the problem, but had very little success, until we heard about Stephano Carrini's death in Barcelona."

"Over the heroin."

"Heroin? Heavens no. They shot him so he could serve as transport."

"Oh."

"We keep very careful track of deaths here." The professor waved to the shelves behind him. "We have a staff of five, upstairs, who read newspapers in every major language. They record all significant deaths, for our analysis. We discovered long ago that death means money. So to speak."

"Yes."

"So when we found out about Carrini's death, we knew what was going on. Tex went down to the Costa Brava to keep track of the people—group 2, according to our calculations."

"Who is group 1?"

"We are," the professor said. "As representatives of Tex."

"And the third group?"

"The count."

"Ah. The count."

The professor smiled happily. "It all fits together, doesn't it?"

"Yes," Ross said.

"But now that you understand everything, I'm sure you see why we need your help. We must discover what happened to the body." He pointed to the map. "We know that the body was taken by hearse from here, in Barcelona, to Lérida, here. That is on the main road to Madrid. At Madrid, the chances are roughly 9,470 to 1 that it would be flown out by plane. Of course, they could go north from Zaragoza to San Sebastián, but that is highly unlikely, as you can see by the odds."

He paused and smoothed his tie, caressing the nude. "Now then. From Lérida, the hearse traveled to Bujaraloz, a little town halfway to Zaragoza. Through a mix-up, we obtained no confirmation that the hearse reached Zaragoza, but we think it did. In fact, we think it got all the way to Guadalajara, sixty miles from Madrid. We're awaiting word on that."

"And what happened at Guadalajara?"

"The hearse disappeared."

"Disappeared?"

"Not actually, of course. But for all practical purposes. We have made a few preliminary calculations and believe that it will be found abandoned here, in Sacedon, south of Guadalajara. The corpse will naturally be gone."

"Yes."

"It stands to reason. The probabilities work out to about 0.747. That's only slide-rule accuracy, but it will do for the moment."

Ross nodded.

"For the present, however, we need more information. The principal question involves a determination of which group did the hijacking."

"Is there any question?" Ross asked.

"Certainly there is," the professor said, with an impatient wave. "We can only rule out group 1, ourselves. Group 2 is possible."

"But they arranged the hearse in the first place."

"Precisely. But they are a difficult group, dissident and argumentative. A falling out within the ranks is quite possible: one chance in seventeen."

"I see."

"Or alternatively, it could have been the work of group 3."

"The count."

"Precisely. The count. And then, as long shots, we must consider any other groups."

"Such as?"

"Such as the undertakers who were hired for the transport job. They might have got wind of what was happening."

"Possible," Ross said.

"Yes, possible. But not likely. One chance in twenty-four thousand. Of course, wars have been won on less..." He sighed. "Mathematics is a cruel taskmaster. But I wander from the main point and the reason for bringing you here. Let me ask you frankly, Dr. Ross. What is your interest in this matter?"

"My interest?" Ross laughed. "Staying alive, I think."

"You have no...vested interest?"

"No," Ross said. "As far as I'm concerned, I came to Spain for a vacation, and I became involved in a mess. I was forced to do an autopsy—"

The professor looked at him sternly. "I trust," he said, "that you *did* insert it into the body."

"Yes," Ross said. "Whatever it was."

"You don't know?" The professor cocked an eyebrow.

"No," Ross said. "Isn't that obvious?"

"You don't know!"

The professor leaped up and danced about the room. "You don't know! You don't know!"

He ran down the room and threw open the door. "Jackman! Tex! He doesn't know!"

"I told you that," Tex said.

"Yes, I know, but… Oh, this is *wonderful* news!"

He ran back to Ross and shook his hand warmly.

"My dear sir, wonderful, wonderful. I can hardly believe my ears."

He sat down, his great bulk shaking with excitement. "You must tell me everything. Absolutely everything."

Ross looked at him steadily. The room fell into silence. Then Ross said, quite loudly and distinctly, "No."

11. THE PROBABILITY OF DEATH

The professor rocked back: "No?"

"No."

"But my dear Doctor, how can you say that?"

"Very easily," Ross said. "I open my mouth, move my tongue, and phonate in such a way as to—"

"No, no," the professor said, with an impatient wave of his hand. "I don't mean that. I mean, have you considered the stakes?"

"I haven't got any idea what they are."

"Precisely. Precisely. You want to stay alive, don't you?"

Ross sighed. "Are you threatening me?"

"Certainly not."

"Why don't you? Everyone else has."

"Dear me, no. I simply meant, have you considered the odds?"

"On what?"

"Staying alive." He stood up. "Here, I'll work them out."

He went to one of the drawing boards, found a sheet of paper and a slide rule. He began to mutter about transformations and Fourier determinants. Occasionally, as he got his answers, he made little grunting sounds.

"Listen," Ross said. "This is silly. I don't want any part of this."

"Ummm," said the professor, working his slide rule.

"I just want to know what's going on. I think I have that right. I've been pushed and bullied, forced to do an autopsy,

beaten up, kidnapped. I think it's time I got some information."

"Umm," the professor said, coming back with a sheet of
figures in his hand. "Quite understandable. Speaking gener-
ally, of course. You're curious. Quite understandable. But,"
he said, frowning at the paper, "not wise."

Ross waited.

"I've computed your probability of survival for a six-month
period. I worked it on age thirty, because it was easier—round
numbers, you know—and because it won't make much dif-
ference. Age-dependent factors are quite minor. So: here
we have the results. Your chances of surviving half a year."

"Go on."

"I should mention, of course, that this is an averaged
result. In other words, your chances of dying within the next
day, or the next week, are quite high. If you survive a month,
the probability of death drops quite sharply. You follow
me?"

"Yes."

"Well then. Here we are. Your chances of survival are
0.443. In other words, you have less than one chance in two
of living until December." The professor shook his head
sadly. "However," he said, "there is one ray of hope. Your
optimum-path probability of survival is much higher. It is, to
be exact, 0.879. Roughly nine chances out of ten of surviving."

"Optimum path?" Ross said.

"Yes. We mean by that, your chances of survival if you do
everything right in the next six months."

"I find this fascinating," Ross said.

"I thought you might."

"And how, may I ask, do I do everything right?"

The professor smiled broadly. "By taking good advice, of course."

"Good advice?"

"My advice," the professor said.

"And this will improve my chances of survival?"

"It will double them," the professor said. "But that is only what you would expect. For example, if you had money to invest in the stock market, would you do so without consulting a skilled broker? You might, but your chances of success would be greater with professional advice."

"We're not talking about stocks," Ross protested. "We're talking about me."

"I regret to say that the mathematics are the same in either instance."

Ross frowned for a moment. "And in order to get your excellent advice…"

The professor nodded and smiled. "Precisely."

He sighed. "All right. I'll tell you everything."

He did, beginning at the start, with the little man on the beach; then the pallbearers; Tex; the autopsy; the trip to Barcelona; the girl in her room.

The professor listened without interrupting. Then he said, "The girl: what did she tell you?"

"She said it had to do with the 'Marriage of Cortez.'"

"I see. What else?"

"That she knew what had been sewn inside the body. And that she had overheard the men talking about taking the shipment to Portugal."

"Portugal! Good God, Portugal! How extraordinary."

"That was what she said."

"Anything further?"

"No, not really."

"Then what?"

He described the knock at the door, and the boiling water, and his wait in the kitchen, and then the girl, unconscious.

"She wasn't dead?"

"No."

"You're quite certain?"

"Yes."

"Please continue."

He then described the meeting with the little blonde who had hidden him from the police. The professor seemed wholly uninterested in this incident and listened impatiently. His interest revived, however, when he described his kidnapping in Barcelona.

"They gave you sodium amytal?"

"That's what they said."

"And you told them everything?"

"I assume I did. I can't really be sure."

"Hmmm," the professor said. "Of course, it doesn't matter one way or the other. Now then: describe the way they died."

"I didn't see it happen. I just woke up and found them all dead."

"But describe them."

Ross shrugged. "Blood streaked all over the walls and ceiling. And they were all—"

"Excuse me," the professor interrupted. "You said blood was streaked over the *ceiling*?"

"Yes."

"How high was the ceiling?"

"About nine feet or so."

"Continue," he said, nodding.

"The men themselves had been slashed. Their clothes

were slashed, and their bodies were slashed. Cut to ribbons by a very sharp knife. Probably a curved knife."

"Why do you say that?"

"Because there was a ripping and a tearing associated. Like a curved knife had gotten under the skin and then torn upward."

"Interesting. Further details?"

"None, really."

"You mentioned something earlier about a smell in the room."

"Yes," Ross said. "I didn't notice it, but Carrini did. They told him it was some kind of free aftershave lotion. A sample that was being given out."

"How bizarre. What do you make of it?"

"Nothing," Ross said.

"Neither do I. Continue."

Ross shrugged. "That's all."

The professor stared at the floor for a long time. His lips moved but he did not speak. Finally he said, "It all fits, except for Portugal. That is a nasty shock, Portugal. Quite a nasty shock. I would never have suspected them of it."

"Who?"

"Well now," the professor said. "You have fulfilled your half of the bargain. And I promised to keep you alive in return."

"Something like that."

"Very well. It's quite simple, really. There are only two countries you cannot be in. Spain and France. And, of course, now Portugal as well. You must go somewhere else, and I have just the place."

"You do?"

"The Canary Islands," the professor said. "Marvelous this time of year, very relaxing. Shall I get you a ticket?"

"Two tickets," Ross said.

"Fine. You can fly directly from Orly airport."

Ross shook his head. "No. I have to go back to Barcelona."

"Dear me. I wouldn't advise it, really. Much too dangerous."

"I'm going."

The professor shrugged. "As you wish. But I warned you…"

"You can have two tickets waiting for me at the Barcelona airport," Ross said.

"Very well," the professor said. "I hope you make it."

"I will."

"Ummm," the professor said.

They stood and walked out of the room. In the anteroom, Tex was waiting with Jackman. Tex looked at his watch.

"Just time to make the four o'clock plane."

Ross said, "We're leaving now?"

"Of course. Wouldn't want to keep a fine woman like that waiting, would you?"

The professor smiled kindly. "You were so nice to visit us, Dr. Ross. I wish you luck."

They shook hands. Tex and Ross went to the door.

"Oh, one thing," the professor said.

Ross stopped. "Yes?"

"You might be interested to know that Stephano Carrini has no brother. No living relatives of any kind, in fact. Not that it matters to him. He is presently living quite happily—in Argentina. Just thought you'd like to know."

When they were alone, Jackman said to the professor, "How did the interview go?"

"Very well. The man is a simple, naïve fool. I could hardly believe a man could be such a fool and also a doctor."

"He talked."

The professor sighed. "Yes. Beautifully."

A blonde girl entered from another room.

"Ah, Karin," the professor said. "My congratulations. You did an excellent job."

"Thank you, Professor."

"You were quite convincing. He believes the Portugal business implicitly."

"And he will tell the count?"

"Oh yes. He will."

Jackman said, "How did you get him to talk?"

"I convinced him," the professor said, "with a cock-and-bull story about his chances of survival."

"And he believed it?"

"Yes. Terribly naïve. It's depressing."

Jackman looked out the window and watched as Ross and Tex got into a taxi.

Karin said, "What are his chances of survival, Professor?"

The professor gave a light smile and caressed his tie.

"Zero," he said. "Absolute zero."

12. GETTING OUT

Their airplane landed as darkness fell. Ross walked with Tex through customs, then they shook hands.

"Your tickets," Tex said, "for the Canary Islands will be waiting for you tomorrow morning. Aero Travel Agency."

"Good," Ross said.

"I'd be careful tonight," Tex said.

"I will."

"Good luck, then."

"Thanks," Ross said.

With a casual wave, Tex left him. Ross caught a taxi.

"Where have you been?" She rolled over in the darkness. "I've been worried."

"Paris," he said.

"If you're not going to be serious—"

"Paris. Really."

She sat up in bed. "Paris? There and back?"

"Yes."

"Why?"

"I didn't have any choice. I'm surrounded by lunatics these days."

He told her the story briefly and told her about the tickets.

"We're getting out," he said.

She smiled in the darkness. "I'm glad," she said.

He finished undressing and lay down beside her. She put her head on his shoulder. He felt dampness.

"What's the matter?"

"I was worried. I really was."

He stroked her hair. "It's all right."

"You shouldn't do things like that to me."

He laughed. "I didn't know you cared."

"You know it now."

"Yes," he said, "I guess I do."

She was silent for a moment, then said, "Anything could have happened. You're such an innocent guy."

"Me? Innocent?"

"Yes. You."

"No, I'm tough and wicked. Hardened, world-weary…"

"Stop it." She kissed him. He tasted salt.

He felt her body move up against him, soft and sleepy-warm. She locked her legs around him.

Later, she smoked a cigarette and said, "I know why I missed you."

"It's just sex. That's all we have between us," Ross said cheerfully.

"It is, right now. And you'd better tell it to behave."

"It has a mind of its own."

"You must be exhausted," she said.

"No," he said.

"You're a fool," she said, touching him.

"Yes," he said.

"You're an innocent.'"

"Yes."

"You're so strong."

"Yes."

"I love you," she said.

"Yes," he said.

❁

The morning was bright, sunny, and cheerful. They had breakfast in the room and joked as they packed their bags. Angela talked excitedly of the Canary Islands; she had never been; she was eager to see them; she had heard the beaches were black sand and marvelous.

An hour before the flight, Ross called down to the desk for a porter to take their bags. Five minutes passed and there was a knock on the door. Angela was in the bathroom, combing her hair.

"That must be the porter," she called.

Ross opened the door.

A man walked into the room, a small, thin, dark-skinned man, looking very pale.

"You are Ross," he said. He was very short of breath. He leaned against the door.

"Yes," Ross said.

"I must talk to you. I am...I am...Hamid..."

"What do you want?" The man seemed to be in pain, great pain. He was gasping for breath and grimacing.

"You are the only one I can trust. You must listen. It went according to plan. Everything. I was driving...on the road to Malaga...and then I knew I was followed. So I hid it. Both of them. And now..."

"Hid what?"

"You must listen," he said. "There is no time. I stole the body and hid them. One is near the Washington Irving, twenty paces east. The other is near the lions, down low, by the water. Listen..."

He coughed, a long, hacking cough.

"Are you all right?"

"Yes, Doctor. Listen...remember carefully: Washington Irving, and the lions. Remember. One is real, and the other—"

He stopped, shuddered twice, and coughed blood. Then he seemed to suffer a great and final pain. He toppled forward onto the floor. The door he had been leaning against was covered with blood.

Ross looked down at the man's back. It had been cut and shredded, gouged deep, the flesh and bones exposed. He turned the man over and stared at the lifeless face.

Angela came out, and screamed.

He felt for a pulse and found none. And he remembered lifting an eyelid and seeing that the eye did not move; it was rolled backward.

Angela was still screaming. She screamed for a very long time.

13. THE CELL

The police were very polite as they showed him to his cell. It was small, reasonably clean, and not too damp; the bed, however, was almost soggy. He was locked in and left alone with his thoughts for half an hour. Then a trim, erect man with a neatly clipped moustache came up.

"Good evening." He gave a slight, formal bow. "Capitán Gonzales, *Guardia Civil*."

"Hello," Ross said.

Capitán Gonzales let himself into the cell, locked it, and leaned against the bars.

"You are Dr. Ross."

"Yes."

"You may be interested to know that the medical examination has been completed."

"And?"

"The diagnosis was death from internal hemorrhage, secondary to puncture of liver and kidney by a posterior approach. Done by some kind of sharp instrument. The coroner suggested it might have been a scalpel, since the blade was apparently rather short."

"I see."

"Do you wish to confess now?"

"No," Ross said. "I have nothing to confess."

Capitán Gonzales sighed. "Why is it always the foreigners?" he said, almost to himself. "I am beginning to think that Americans come to Spain specifically to kill or be killed."

"It's the in country for killing," Ross said. "Just a fashion. It'll pass in a year or so."

"You are not amusing."

"I didn't think you'd like it. But then, I don't like being arrested."

"And we," Gonzales said, "do not like murder."

"There. You see? Nobody's happy."

Gonzales said, "Did you know the man?"

"Never saw him before in my life."

"Do you possess a scalpel?"

"No. I am a radiologist."

"So you say."

"Yes," Ross said. "So I say."

"But you told the officer who made the arrest that you were on your way to the Canary Islands."

"That's true. I was. I had called the desk for a bellboy, and—"

"You were checking out of the hotel?"

"Yes. I was on my way to the Canary Islands."

"Were you?"

"Of course."

"How did you intend to go?"

"By plane. There is a nine o'clock flight—"

"No."

"No?"

Gonzales shook his head. "There is only one flight each day, and that is at noon."

"But there must be—"

"Do you have tickets?"

"No. I told the officer that my tickets were being held at the Aero Travel Agency."

Gonzales sighed. "You know," he said, "I am not a genius, Doctor."

"I never said you were."

"What I mean," Gonzales said, "is that though I am not a genius, you must be an idiot. Because it is all quite simple to me."

"Oh?"

"Yes. You are lying through your teeth."

"Why do you say that?"

"Because," Gonzales said, "You had no tickets for a flight to the Canary Islands."

"Look," Ross said, "there must be some mistake. I thought it was a nine o'clock flight, but I could have been confused. It could have been a noon flight, and—"

He stopped.

Gonzales was shaking his head.

"Why are you so sure?"

"Because," Gonzales said, "there is no Aero Travel Agency."

"But there must be."

"There is not."

"But I was told—"

He stopped. Things were bad enough without telling Gonzales everything. If he told them everything, he would either be committed to an institution or summarily hung.

Gonzales said, "Told by whom?"

"No one. Forget it."

"You know," Gonzales said, "it is said in Spain that Americans are bad liars. But really, doctor, you surpass all my expectations."

"Thank you very much."

"You are really quite impossible."

Ross said, "Flattery will get you nowhere."

"You still will not make a confession?"

"Of course not."

"We can wait," Gonzales said.

"You can't hold me. You have no proof."

Gonzales smiled grimly. "This is Spain."

"I want to see a lawyer from the consulate."

"One is coming. We always notify the consulate in these cases."

"You'll let me see a lawyer, then?"

"Perhaps. Perhaps not."

He finished his cigarette, dropped it to the floor, and ground it out under his boot heel.

"In the meantime, I will leave you alone, to think. When I return, I will expect answers. Understand?"

As he unlocked the door and let himself out, Ross said, "There won't be any answers."

"There had better be," Gonzales said.

He left.

The consulate man was young, with a crew cut and a nervous manner.

"Charlie Sweet," he said, extending a damp hand. "How are you?"

"Great," Ross said.

"They treating you all right? I'll make a formal complaint if they're not."

"They're treating me fine."

"Ah, that's good." He sighed in relief. "Anything I can do for you? Want cigarettes? Candy? Newspapers from home? It can all be arranged."

"I want out," Ross said.

"I'm sure you do. But it's really not a bad cell. I've seen worse."

"That's encouraging."

"I've talked with the consul about your case," Charlie said.

"The consul has conferred by phone with the ambassador. He's not in Madrid now; he's in San Sebastián, since the capital moves in the summer. To San Sebastián."

"And?"

"I just wanted you to know, the government is doing everything possible, sparing no expense. It's expensive to call from Barcelona to San Sebastián."

"What did the consul and the ambassador say?"

"Well, they agree it's serious."

"I could have told them that."

"Then too," Charlie said, "I've talked with the police here. They've described the charges, and given me some idea of the nature of the evidence."

"Yes?"

"Take my advice," Charlie said. "Confess now."

"But I'm not guilty."

"The trouble," Charlie said, "is that the prisons are over-crowded. If you're convicted and you put up a fight, they may ship you to a political prison. They're terrible. On the other hand, if you confess, you'll go to a civil prison, which is much nicer. And with any luck, we may be able to get you out in five or ten years."

"That's encouraging."

"You're young," Charlie said. "Five or ten years won't be too bad. Think of it that way."

"I'd rather not think of it at all."

"It's the best we can do, I'm afraid. You must deal with realities."

"The reality," Ross said, "is that I'm not guilty."

"Come on, now," Charlie said, with a man-to-man grin, "you don't need to act like that around me. I don't know what you're involved in, but there's no sense pretending, is there?"

"Christ," Ross said.

"It's up to you," Charlie said. "Whenever you decide to confess, you can call for the guard. He'll bring writing things."

"Listen," Ross said, standing up. "Can't you understand? I'm not guilty, and I want to get out of here."

Charlie sighed and stood up. "You'll come around. I've tried to reason with you, God knows." He stepped to the bars and banged on them until a guard came down. "Just remember," he said. "Any time you want anything, give us a call. Cigarettes, magazines, anything. We'll be in touch. Good luck."

He left.

Ross stood, dumbfounded, for a long time.

Then he sat down on the damp cot and thought. He thought about everything, from the very beginning, from the moment he arrived in Spain. He thought about every person he had met, every conversation he had had.

And slowly, painfully, he began to put it together.

Part III

"Radiologists have the shortest lifespan of all medical specialists."
— U.S. Bureau of Medical Statistics

Part III

PROLOGUE

He was a big man, shouldering his way through the darkness, his face concealed beneath the broad hat. He hummed to himself as he walked along the Barcelona waterfront, down dark streets which smelled of fish and urine, a lonely and quiet part of town. But he was walking quickly, because he had to meet someone.

He was far from the red-light district, and so he was surprised when the girl appeared, stepping out from a doorway in front of him. Even in the dark, he could see she had short blonde hair and a trim body; she stood lewdly, with one hand on her hip.

"Howdy," he said.

"Interest you?" she said.

He paused in amazement. "You're American?"

"Americans for Americans," she said, and stepped close, standing on her tiptoes to kiss him. Gently, he pushed her away.

"I'd sure like to," he said. "But I can't."

She pouted. "I'll give you a bargain price."

"I'd sure like to…"

She kissed him again.

"Nice perfume," he said, hesitating. He was thinking that he was late for the meeting already, ten minutes late, and yet…

"I'm glad you like it," she said.

She kissed him and put her arm behind his neck. He felt something damp: sweaty hands. That tore it. He hated a woman, even a pretty woman, with sweaty hands.

He broke away. "I'm awful sorry," he said, "but I've got
to go."

And he left her, standing in the alley. He looked back once
and glimpsed her, still standing and watching him. Then he
turned the corner and was alone once more with the smells
and the night.

As he walked, he continued to smell her perfume. It was
too sweet, but sensual in its way, a kind of heady, strong
aroma. It seemed to cling to him, but perhaps he was imag-
ining that.

He had walked another block when it happened. Without
warning, something fell on him, knocking him down, cutting
his face in an instant of sharp, searing pain. He grunted and
rolled over, feeling a flapping and a musty breeze around
him.

A bird.

He kicked and scrambled to his feet. When he stood, he
was alone in the street, with blood pouring down from a cut
on his head. He looked around, then up.

It happened again. He saw it coming, a giant bird with
the wings folded tight to the body, crashing down on him
like a missile, and he tried to duck away, but it struck him
in the throat, and he felt himself falling, and then he felt
nothing at all.

14. PNGed

Peter Ross awoke in the morning feeling damp, stiff, and unrested. He looked up and saw a guard unlocking his door. His first thought was that they were bringing him breakfast, and then Capitán Gonzales walked in.

Ross was not really surprised to see him.

"Get up," Gonzales said.

Ross got up slowly.

"You are very lucky," Gonzales said. "We had scheduled interrogation to begin this morning. Before breakfast. That is so you would not be sick."

"Thoughtful of you."

"But there will be no interrogation."

"I know," Ross said.

"I suspected you did," Gonzales said. "Those with powerful friends always know."

"That's me," Ross said. "A man with powerful friends."

"You are lucky," Gonzales repeated. "If it had been the consulate, they could have done nothing."

"But it wasn't the consulate," Ross said.

"No."

"Tell me," Ross said. "Which of my many powerful friends was it?"

Gonzales shook his head.

"But I have to send a thank-you note."

Gonzales spat on the floor. "The judge was paid. The charges are dismissed. That is all you need to know."

He led Ross down a corridor, toward the exit.

"The government," he said, "is processing the necessary papers to declare you *persona non grata*. In less than forty-eight hours, you will be forced to leave Spain. I suggest you avoid unpleasantness and leave first."

"Believe me," Ross said, "I will."

"Forgive me," Gonzales said, "for doubting you."

He opened the door, and Ross stepped out into the sunlight. Gonzales gave him a final, strange look, and closed the door.

Ross was alone, and free.

He took a taxi to his hotel, where the concierge greeted him like a man returned from the dead. "Ah, Señor, she will be very glad to see you."

"She is still here?"

"Yes, Señor."

"That's interesting," Ross said. He was not surprised. He took the elevator to the top floor and unlocked the door to the room. Angela was sitting on the bed, reading a paperback and munching an apple. She threw them down when she saw him.

"Pete! Thank God."

She ran up and threw her arms around him, hugging him, but he did not respond. After a moment, she stepped back.

"Something wrong?"

"You tell me."

"Pete, I'm so glad to see you. What's the matter?"

"I don't know," he said. He went to the closet and opened it; their suitcases were there, still packed. "Why did you stay here?"

"What a foolish question. I was worried about you, and I—"

"Knew I would be getting out soon?"

"No," she said, in a soft voice. "How would I know that?"

"You tell me."

She came up to him, very gently, and touched his face. "Pete, please—"

He turned away from her. "You know," he said, "I've been thinking. About a lot of things."

"So have I, and—"

"And the more I thought, the more peculiar everything seems."

She stared at him and said nothing. He walked to the window and looked out.

"Because," he said, "somebody has kept track of me from the minute I entered Spain. Somebody has told people where I am, what I'm doing, and where I'm going."

"Pete, if you think—"

"So," he said, "I began to work on it. To try to decide who it was, and why. Especially why."

"I don't understand what you're saying."

"Sure you do. You understand fine."

"If you mean that I've been spying on you—"

"That's right," he said, sitting down.

They said nothing for a long time. Then she sat on the bed, fumbled in her purse, and lit a cigarette.

"Yes," she said. "It's all true."

"You're working for the count?"

"Yes," she said in a soft voice.

"How long?"

"A year. A little more."

Ross turned away in disgust. "Christ," he said. He frowned, looking out the window at the traffic. In the glass, he saw his features reflected—hard, angry, and a little sad.

"It's too bad," he said.

She did not reply.

"I suppose you know all about the autopsy?"

"Yes."

"And what I did?"

"Yes."

"Who told you?"

"The count. He had a spy in the group that arranged the autopsy. It's a long story."

"The count seems to know everything."

She sighed. "Almost."

He turned back and looked at her.

She was huddled on the bed, her skirt pulled up, looking forlorn and tender. He fought an impulse and said, "The count sounds very remarkable. When do I meet him?"

"Whenever you want." Her voice was flat.

"That's why you stayed, isn't it? To take me to him? After he paid off the judge and got me free?"

"Yes."

He looked at her face, tear-stained, pinched. "He must pay you well. Were you really a stewardess, or an actress?"

"I'm not acting."

"Oh. That's good."

"Please, Pete—"

"You really had me fooled."

"I'm not acting."

"Very good, for an amateur."

"Pete, I love you. I swear it."

"I'm sure," he said, "that you would have cried buckets when I received my prison sentence. You would have cried for a week, even. Maybe two."

"You're not fair."

"I'm scared. I don't expect you to understand it. I'm scared."

"So am I."

"Swell. Just so you take me to the count."

She got up wearily from the bed. "You don't have to go," she said. "I could tell him you never returned to the hotel. No one would know."

She wiped her eyes with a handkerchief. The eyes, sad and red, still pleaded with him.

"Too late for that," he said. "I'm in too deep."

"You're not."

"I am, thanks to you. I am now an integral cog in the machinery. I have been primed and filled with information. I am a living set-up."

"What are you talking about?"

"Take me to the count," he said.

"Pete, it's dangerous."

"No kidding."

"Pete, please, stop it. I can't take much more."

"That's good to hear."

She walked up to him then and slapped him as hard as she could. It was not very hard; he blinked. She kicked him in the shin.

"You're a fool, a damn fool! Don't you understand anything? Get out, get out, forget the whole thing!"

He stared at her and watched as she ran her fingers through her glossy black hair.

"Call the count," he said. "Now."

The speedometer on the red Mercedes limousine said one-sixty, and it was calibrated in miles. The car tore across the mountainous dry land, raising a cloud of dust behind. The driver was a squat Spaniard with a heavy beard and wrap-around sunglasses. He said nothing, but drove with determination.

In the back seat, Ross sat with Angela, not speaking. They had been driving for three hours, crossing the same harshly monotonous landscape at the same breakneck speed. Occasionally, he looked at her, and she pretended not to notice and continued to stare out the window.

He wanted to talk to her, to trust her, but he knew he could not. Not now, and perhaps not ever. That was the way it was, and the way it had to be. He still did not understand what was happening, except that he had somehow become crucial in everything. The professor had talked to him, but the professor must have known that Angela was working for the count. Therefore, everything the professor said was calculated to be relayed to the count.

But Hamid—that was another thing altogether. Something quite different. Hamid was somebody's mistake. Whose mistake Ross did not know. But a mistake.

Now Ross was letting himself in for it. A stupid maneuver. Angela was right, he was a damned fool. But he could not help himself. There had been a time when it was all very frightening. And then there was a time when it was all very macabre and confusing. Finally, it had become a roaring pain in the ass. Ross wanted to know how it all fitted together and why he had become involved.

So he was going to see the count.

He was a damned fool, no doubt about it. This was none of his business, it was too deep, too complex, too intricate, too violent. If he had any sense, he'd leave. He'd stop the car right now, and hitch a ride back to the next big city, and take the next plane back to New York. He'd quit and forget it all. After a month in New York, it would all seem like a bad dream, nothing more.

Angela said, "I'm sorry to get you involved."

"It doesn't matter."

"Yes," she said. "It does."

He didn't want to talk to her. When he heard her voice, his stomach twisted, and he felt odd. He wanted to trust her, yet he knew he could not. That was all past. It could not be recaptured.

He stared out the window. They passed a farmhouse, a simple shack surrounded by animals—a lazy burro, clucking chickens, a litter of pigs. The farmhouse stood alone in the desolate landscape. There was no sign of a living person anywhere. And then it was gone, lost in the swirling dust plume of the car.

15. THE COUNT

Late that evening, they came down from the Sierras toward a large city spread across the plains below them. They did not, however, enter the city, but instead headed north, to a rugged area in the outskirts, in the foothills of the mountains.

Ross nodded to the city. "Granada?"

"Yes," Angela said.

"The count lives here?"

"Nearby. It will be a few minutes, no more."

The Mercedes left the main road, and traveled up a twisting dirt track. It was dark, and they seemed to be passing through an orchard or fruit grove of some kind; Ross could not be sure. After several minutes, they came around a bend and saw the castle.

It was nestled into the foothills, a tall, imposing stone building, showing the Moorish influence in its arches and masonry. It was brightly lighted. In front was a circular drive, a pleasant lawn, and a large fountain with splashing water.

The car came to a halt, and they stepped out into the cool night air. Angela led him up the steps to the massive, iron-studded door. She knocked, using a cast iron knocker, which Ross noticed was made in the shape of a human fist.

After a moment, the door was swung back, and Ross faced a huge man. He wore a butler's uniform, tails with a starched white collar. He was not terribly tall—perhaps six-two—but his shoulders were massive, blocking the doorway, and his body was stocky and powerful. In one hand he held a machine gun; it hung casually, by his side.

"Good evening," the man said, touching his neck with his other hand. The voice had a rasping, mechanical quality. Ross looked and saw the black voice box.

"Good evening, Joaquim," Angela said. "We are here to see the count."

"Yes, Madame," Joaquim said, touching his voice box again. "He is expecting you."

With a flourish, Joaquim turned and led them inside. He moved gracefully for such a big man, Ross thought. But he had some peculiar, hook-shaped scars on his hands, very deep. Several, all over his hands. Ross was wondering how he had hurt his neck when Angela whispered, "Knife fight. Two years ago."

"I see."

"The blade went straight through. They didn't think he would live. The count paid for all the operations."

Ross nodded.

"Joaquim is the count's most trusted servant."

"This way, please," Joaquim said. The voice grated, crackling, rebounding off the cold stone walls. Ross looked around the inside of the castle. The rooms and halls were cavernous and chilly, decorated with medieval armor, weapons, and tapestries. He felt as if he had stepped into another century, another era.

There was no electric lighting in this section of the castle; smoking torches burned from high brackets near the ceiling, and Joaquim, walking ahead of them, cast a long shadow. They followed him down endless passages, cold, slightly damp, and depressing, until at last they came to a long open room. It had once been a banquet hall; the ceiling was high and elaborately carved and inlaid with gold. However, there was no long table. Instead, there were hard wooden chairs and benches, and rushes on the stone floor.

At the far end, barely visible in the flickering yellow torchlight, was a heavy, ancient desk. Behind it, in a dark chair, sat a man, writing. He looked up as they entered.

"Your visitors, sir," said Joaquim.

The man smiled. He had a full beard and close-cropped dark hair. He wore a blue blazer and a wine-red sweater underneath. His face was oddly childish.

"Good, good."

When he spoke, his voice was high and squeaky, like the voice of a young girl.

Angela and Ross moved forward, down the long hall. Their footsteps were muffled by the rushes. In a corner, a large Doberman pinscher growled, but the count waved his hand irritably, and the dog subsided.

Ross approached, and Angela said, "The Count of Navarre. Dr. Ross."

"I am glad," the count said, stroking his beard, "to meet you at last."

And then he stood, and Ross saw: the Count of Navarre was a dwarf.

"A shock, I suppose," the count said, coming around the desk and walking up to Ross. He held his hand up to shake, and Ross bent slightly to take it. "It always is a shock," the count said, "Uncomfortable, but there it is."

He turned to Angela, who bent over so she could be kissed on both cheeks.

"How are you, my dear?"

"Fine, just fine." She smiled.

"Good. And you brought the good doctor. There was no trouble with the police?"

"No," Ross said. "Thanks for getting me out."

The count shrugged. "My pleasure. How do you like the castle?"

Ross found it cold and gloomy and depressing, but he said, "Very interesting."

"I have tried to preserve it," the count said, "as best I could. I feel a strong link to my ancestors and wish to maintain the surroundings. Even my...stature. Small people have always been associated with the Spanish court. You have seen 'Los Niños'?"

"Yes," Ross lied.

"Ah, well, then you know. But come: the house is not all rushes and torches."

The count led the way out of the room. Near the fireplace, the Doberman roused himself and growled again.

"Quiet, Franco," said the count.

The dog was silent.

"An amusing name for a dog, do you think? And so well trained."

He led them down another corridor, past a door, and suddenly they were in a large, very modern room. The walls were whitewashed, the furniture Scandinavian, the lighting electric. Everything was built low; Ross noticed that the legs on the couches and chairs had been cut to make them even lower.

"Please sit," the count said, dropping into a chair. He clapped his hands, and Joaquim appeared. "What will you drink?"

"Scotch," Ross said.

Angela nodded.

"Two double Scotches," the count said, "and a brandy with soda for me."

"Of course, sir," Joaquim rasped, and left.

"I keep a part of the castle modern," the count said, waving to the room. "In a sense, you could say I live in two worlds. But that is the fate of all nobility. We are outmoded, living relics. Our very names are fossils. Doctor, will you be my guest for the next few days?"

Ross shrugged.

"I think you will enjoy it," the count said. "And I intend you no harm."

"I think you ought to know," Ross said, "that within forty-eight hours, I will be declared *persona non grata* in Spain."

The count laughed delightedly. "PNGed, as they say in diplomatic circles. Wonderful." He looked at Angela: "You're very quiet, my dear."

"I'm tired."

"We've had a little argument," Ross said.

The count laughed, a high, squeaking child's laugh. "An argument with Angela? How absurd."

"I realized she knew what was going on."

"Oh," the count said, "Angela knows nothing. In fact, she knows less than you."

"Impossible," Ross said. "Nobody knows less than me."

The count laughed again. "You have a sense of humor."

"I'm learning to lose it."

"No doubt, no doubt. This must have been a very trying experience for you. But it will all be explained shortly."

"That's good."

"I can see you don't believe me. That is your prerogative. But you have mistreated a very fine girl and you should apologize."

The drinks came.

"Later," Ross said.

The count turned to Angela. "Is he always so hostile?"

"No," she said.

"Let's say I'm confused," Ross said.

"All in good time," the count said. He raised his glass. "*Salud*."

"*Salud*."

Ross sniffed his drink. "I suppose this is poisoned," he said.

"I suppose," the count said, nodding. And then he laughed. "You Americans," he said. "So morbid."

He sipped his drink, smacked his lips, and said, "Well now. You're undoubtedly hungry. Dinner will be served in twenty minutes. In the meantime, would you care to see my collection?"

"Why not?" Ross said, wondering what kind of collection it was.

"Good," the count said. "Come along."

On the way, he showed them their quarters. Two rooms along a long corridor. Each was stunning in its simplicity and its blending of Spanish antiques with modern furniture. Then he led them into the largest bathroom Ross had ever seen.

It was the size of a large living room, and it adjoined the count's own bedroom, also large. The bathroom was done in Perugina marble, white with veins of gold. The tub was eight feet long and sunken, the sink and mirror were equally large, but the majority of the room was given over to shelves. Along the shelves were bottles of all shapes and sizes, colors and descriptions. Ross looked: it was like a library of bottles, like an old apothecary shop.

"What are they?"

"Aftershave lotions," the count said gravely, "and cologne.

You are looking at the finest collection of cologne in the world. Five hundred and forty-seven different varieties, at last count, though I now have the Givenchy line, which increases the number somewhat. Look here." He removed a bottle.

"This was made up specially, from an old formula. It is an exact duplicate of the cologne that Cortez was known to have favored. Smell it."

Ross bent over and sniffed the opened bottle. It smelled like furniture polish.

"Not very elegant, eh?" The count laughed. "No sophistication in those days, no ability to blend and meld the spices. What you smell is a very heavy lemon oil extract. It was in vogue then. Try this."

Another bottle was pushed under Ross's nose.

"From the court of Henry VIII. Wintergreen and cinnamon, essentially. Unusual, but interesting. Of course, Henry used it because he thought it was an aphrodisiac. Poor man. He needed one."

The bottle was replaced on the shelf, and a new one selected, a slim green flask with a ground glass stopper.

"Now this," said the count, opening it with a flourish, "is a great rarity. It was used during the time of the Medicis, in Florence. An alcohol solution of *cantharis vesicatoria*, with oil of wintergreen and crushed orchids to give the proper odor. The basic ingredient, of course, is derived from the dried bodies of Spanish flies."

"I see."

"Russian flies, too, for that matter. Popularly regarded as an aphrodisiac. Absorbed through the skin, you see, but only useful if applied topically to the appropriate areas. The nether regions, as it were."

He waved the bottle under Ross and put it back.

"The collection goes on. Most of them have been made specially for me. There is, for instance, a selection from Abdul of Cairo—do you know him?—the marvelous magician of scents in that part of the world. Very subtle, indeed. And, too, I have all the standard commercial varieties."

"Fascinating," Ross said.

"A hobby. A mere hobby. But it passes the time. Naturally, I also have a collection of gems, prized stones which have been in the family for centuries. That is, of course, the heart of the matter."

"Of course."

"I can explain further," the count said, "at dinner." He reached for a bottle, a small, squat, purple jar with a cork stopper, opened it, and handed it to Angela.

"What is it?"

"A widely used item in Spain during the latter half of the sixteenth century. It was manufactured by the royal perfumers in Seville. Called 'Remorse.' It was used by leading ladies of the day. The story is that it will ensnare the heart of a loved one who seems to be drifting away."

Angela took the bottle, and poured a few drops into her palm. Then, looking directly at Ross, she rubbed it behind her ears and over her neck.

"I don't believe it," Ross said.

The count smiled. "We must not always be so contemptuous of the past, Doctor," he said. "We may have the advantages of modern science, but they had the benefit of experience."

With a laugh, he led them to the dining room.

The count pushed his plate away and motioned to Joaquim for more wine. As the glasses were refilled, he said, "The story you wish to hear begins a long time ago. To start it, I must go back to my most famous ancestor."

"Who is that?" Ross said.

The count lifted his wineglass, holding it thoughtfully to the light. "Montezuma," he said. He looked over at Ross. "That surprises you? Montezuma had many children, and two—a son and a daughter—embraced Christianity. They came to Spain and founded noble houses here. That was more than four hundred and fifty years ago."

Ross nodded.

"Montezuma," the count said, in a low voice. "You must imagine him. A tall, thin man of forty, with a palace in the jungle so vast, so huge that the conquistadors became exhausted walking through it. No Spaniard ever saw it all. Montezuma had a thousand wives, of which two were lawful, and no one knew how many children he had. He had become king of Mexico at twenty-three and his power was absolute. It was said that he could change his sex from male to female if he wished. The rumors, the stories, the fables of his power were endless. And his treasure was vast.

"When he died at the age of forty-one of battle wounds, the looting of his treasure had already begun. According to a prior agreement, one-fifth of all booty was sent directly to Charles V, King of Spain. Cortez sent off two shiploads of booty with a letter dated Cojohuacan, May 15, 1522. That shipment was very important. Very important. It is a story told in bloodshed—bloodshed which continues to this very day."

The count drank his wine in an impulsive gesture, as a child might. He wiped his mouth delicately with a handkerchief and set the glass down.

"I deplore the bloodshed, naturally, though I recognize the historical parallels. The stakes are very great. You have heard of the Emerald of Cortez?"

"No," Ross said.

"In the original accounts, it was said to be cut in the shape of a pyramid, and so large that the base was as broad as a man's palm. This makes it one of the largest emeralds known to exist in the world. Cortez described the stone and sent it to Charles by ship. The ship touched at the Azores and then, en route to Spain, was captured by a French privateer. The stone was found and confiscated. Later, it became part of the crown jewels of Francis I, His Most Christian Majesty. Christian, but not above a little thievery. An honored religious custom."

The count frowned and twisted his empty wineglass in his hand.

"And then?" Ross said.

"The jewel remained in France until the Revolution in 1789. Then it was lost and presumably destroyed. Historians have long felt that some petty merchant came into possession of the emerald and, not recognizing its historical value, broke it down to make a number of smaller gems."

"I see."

"However, there have always been rumors that the stone still existed intact. My family has followed those rumors faithfully for generations. At one time, the stone was thought to be in Copenhagen, and then to be lost in a fire. Fifty years later, it was reported in Vienna. My grandfather tracked it to Switzerland, but died in a rather mysterious rockslide before he could recover the gem. And there the story ended. Until last month."

"What happened then?"

"Last month," the count said, "I heard that a very large emerald in the shape of a pyramid had been stolen by a Neapolitan from a wealthy Greek living in Capri. The stone was sold on the black market to a Genoese merchant. I made the proper inquiries and found my efforts crowned with success."

"You obtained the stone."

"Yes. I hired a team of four rather disreputable gentlemen to manage transport. I took this precaution because I had heard that an eccentric in Paris was also attempting to obtain the stone."

"The professor."

"Yes," he said. "The professor. You've been to see him, of course, and he has filled you with all sorts of nonsense, knowing that it would eventually get back to me. I'm not interested in any of it. You see, the professor and I have been playing a game of wits. He is immensely clever, if I say so myself."

He smiled slightly.

"I heard that the professor was arranging purchase for a buyer in America."

"Tex?"

"Heavens no," the count said. "Tex is a cheap hood, his hired assassin. Was, that is."

"He's dead?"

"I assume so," the count said carefully. "You see, Tex was all part of the professor's plan to sidetrack me. And Carrini— that wasn't his real name, of course—was part of my plan. Carrini was pretending to prepare the emerald for shipment to America; the autopsy was planned out in great detail. I knew that the professor would get word of this and that it would throw him off. He would naturally assume that Carrini, my hired agent, was double-crossing me."

"But he wasn't."

"No indeed. He was following orders."

"Why was he killed?"

The count sighed. "That was a sad mistake. When the body

was stolen, I assumed that Carrini had done in fact what he was doing in pretense. I did not know then that it was all Hamid's fault."

"I'm getting confused," Ross said.

"Understandable. You see, Hamid was the driver of the hearse. He was supposed to 'steal' the body and deliver it to me. But the professor had apparently anticipated my ruse and had bribed Hamid."

"Then Hamid did not deliver the emerald to you?"

"No," the count said, frowning. "As you know perfectly well."

Ross shook his head. "I don't know anything. This is all screwy as hell."

"On the contrary. It is quite logical. A game of chess between the professor and myself."

"I never was any good at chess."

"You may learn quickly," the count said, "under stress." He turned to Angela and glanced at his watch. "It's nearly midnight. Are you sure you were followed?"

"Yes," she said. "Quite sure."

Ross frowned. "We were followed?"

"All the way from Barcelona. Two black Peugeots."

"Excellent," the count said. "Then obviously, they do not know."

"Do not know what?" Ross said.

"Where Hamid finally decided to hide the body. You see, he was killed before he could tell them."

"Who killed him?"

The count shrugged. "Difficult to say."

"The police said it was done with a scalpel."

When the count heard this, he laughed very hard. "A scalpel? Did they really? How frightfully amusing."

Ross looked over at Angela. She was watching the count, watching his laugh. Her face was pale.

"The police," the count said, "are not very intelligent. As a rule. But we digress from the crucial point."

"Which is?"

"Which is that you talked with Hamid before he died. You, and you alone. I want to know what he told you."

"He told me nothing."

"I don't believe that."

"It's the truth."

The count sighed. "Perhaps. There are ways of telling. As you may know, the castle is equipped with an exemplary dungeon. All the finest equipment from the fifteenth century. It was the time of the Inquisition, and the inventiveness was remarkable. We can discuss it in the morning."

Ross got up from the table. "I appreciate your hospitality," he said, "and your threats."

"Not threats, Doctor. I bear you no grudge. But you must understand I want that stone—my ancestors have sought it for centuries, and now at last, it is within my grasp. The culmination of a search lasting hundreds of years is about to come to an end. It is an exciting prospect, a marvelous prospect. I am eager to finish at last."

"And desperate," Ross said.

"Yes, desperate. Desperate as any man alive. I mean to have that stone, Doctor. I mean to return it to its rightful place, here, in this castle. And I will not rest until I have succeeded."

He smiled oddly, as if suddenly embarrassed by his outburst. "Well then," he said. "It is late. Can you find your rooms by yourselves?"

"Yes," Angela said.

"Then I bid you both good night and pleasant dreams."

They left, and looking back, Ross had a final glimpse of the little man, with his black beard and his incongruous child's face, standing by the long dining room table in the vast room lighted by flickering candlelight.

Ross sat alone in his room, lying on the bed fully dressed, thinking. The more he thought, the worse things seemed to be. He was quite certain now that the count had killed Carrini and the others. And that he had killed Hamid. How, Ross couldn't imagine—those slashing, bizarre cuts were something out of a nightmare.

But if he had killed so many, he would not hesitate to kill again. Ross had no doubt that the count would kill him, and kill Angela, when it suited him.

And it would suit him just as soon as Ross told him what Hamid had said before he died.

He glanced around his room. It was pleasant, comfortable, appealing, with none of the aspects of a prison. He got up and went to the door, tried it. Unlocked. He shut the door again and returned to the bed.

He wanted a drink. Across the room, on a dark heavy sideboard, were several bottles on a silver tray. He went over, poured three fingers of Scotch, and dropped in an ice cube from a silver ice bucket. He swirled the drink in the glass and wondered what to do.

Then he heard something behind him. He turned. It was Angela, still wearing her dress.

"Would you make me one, too?" she asked.

"Sure." He mixed another.

"Why aren't you in bed?" he said.

"I can't. I'm scared."

"Why?"

"Aren't you scared?"

"No," Ross said. "I rather like the count."

"I used to," Angela said. "Until an hour ago."

Ross gave her the drink. "Listen," he said, "I can save you a lot of trouble."

"How?"

"Instead of making you sit there with a worried face, I'll tell you all I know. Everything Hamid told me. Then you can run down to the count, and you can get to bed early."

"Peter, really—"

"That's why you're here, isn't it?"

"No."

He waited a moment. She said nothing more, but sipped the drink.

"Not very good," he said. "You should have a whole speech prepared. About how frightened you are. About how you no longer like the count. About how you've seen what a heartless little guy he is. You should have a whole thing."

"Peter," she said in a low voice, "I think he's going to kill us."

"Ah, now there's a touch. Nobody's ever tried to kill me before."

"I'm serious. The count will kill us."

"When?"

"As soon as you tell him what you know."

"That will be tomorrow. In the dungeon."

"And he'll kill me."

"Pity."

"I'm serious, Peter."

"So am I."

"Peter, take me away from here."

"Now there's a new one. You want me to lead you to the stone myself. We'll slip out of the castle, slinking around dark corners, and miraculously, we'll make it. Then I'll lead you to the stone, and suddenly, who will appear but the count himself, with voice box alongside. And the machine gun."

"Peter, I swear. I'm serious."

"You keep saying that." Ross went back and made himself another drink. This time he poured five fingers. "You know, I used to be a simple doctor. Just a nice guy, minding my own business, reading X-rays, peddling pills, and sticking needles into people. Making people get well: very simple job. I didn't know anything about gangsters, or professors, or counts, or emeralds."

"Peter."

"You want to know something funny? I've never fired a gun in my life. Not one. Not even in the army. Not even a BB gun. In fact, I haven't even used a slingshot."

"I know him," Angela said. "I've worked for him for nearly a year. I always thought he was basically nice, that his flashes of temper were just…whims. Now I know better."

She stood, standing very straight. She looked at him directly and said, "We have two choices. Either we try to get away tonight, or we wait to get shot in the morning. That's all. Nothing else."

Ross gulped back his drink. "I vote for getting shot. I've been running for a week now. It's tiresome. And exhausting. I hate traveling. I think it's time to get shot."

"I really could have loved you," she said.

"Swell."

"I thought there was something to you. A strength, an inner power. A calmness."

"Nope. Just a show."

She came up to him and stood very close, her hands at her sides. For a long time, she said nothing, and then:

"We had something, Peter."

"My friends call me Dr. Ross."

"We still have something."

"Nope. Just a mistake."

"It's us," she said. "We have something."

"No we don't."

They stared at each other for a long time, and he looked at her eyes, which were very clear and very blue. And something happened. He took her and kissed her hard, until he was out of breath. Finally, he pushed back.

"So I made a mistake," he said. "To err is human."

He looked at her for a long moment, then said, "Let's get the hell out of here."

"Do you trust me?"

"No. I love you."

"Is that different?"

"You bet it is."

"Then kiss me again. I've never been kissed by a man who loved me."

16. ESCAPE

They sat on the bed, and Angela sketched quickly on a pad of paper. Ross drank Scotch—his third, but he felt he needed it. The more Angela talked, the more he felt he needed it.

"We're here," she said, pointing to the sketch, "on the second floor. The count's bedroom is at the far end of the hall, so he won't hear us. We go down these stairs here, and around the corner, and we're on the first floor. That should be simple enough, though when the lights are out, it's very dark."

"Who else is in the house?"

"Joaquim. He sleeps in the west wing, off over here. Along with the other servants: the cook, the maid, and the chauffeur."

"Nobody else at this end?"

"No. Not usually."

"Can we be certain of that?"

"No. We can't be certain of anything."

"All right," he said, looking at the map. "We go down the stairs. Then what?"

"We go to the kitchen, over here."

"Why?"

"Because that's where the keys are. There is a Porsche convertible in the garage. That's the fastest car. We can get the keys in the kitchen, and then slip through the house over to here, and go into the garage."

"Couldn't we go outside? It would be faster and quieter. We could get directly to the garage."

"No," she said.

"Why not?"

"Because of the dog. He's roaming the grounds at night. And the count keeps him hungry in the evenings."

"Nice," Ross said.

"I saw what he did to a burglar once," Angela said. "The man was in the hospital for ten weeks."

"Stop trying to encourage me."

"We'll be safe if we go through the house," she said. "There's only one possible difficulty."

"Yes?"

"The garage doors may have been left open. In that case, the dog may be sleeping inside the garage."

"Can't you charm him?"

"No one can," Angela said, "except the count. Around anyone else, he's vicious."

"Nice."

She folded up the sketch of the house. "Is it all clear?"

"What about the gates out front? Will they be locked?"

"Probably not. We'll have to keep our fingers crossed."

"Okay," Ross said. He stood up. "Let's go." He went to the closet, opened his suitcase, and rummaged through it. "There's one thing that might help us, though."

"What's that?"

"This." He held it up, a thin, metallic tube.

"What is it?"

"Flashlight. For looking down throats. I brought it with me, by accident."

"Lucky," she said.

"So far," he said.

They left the room and tiptoed out into the hall. It was empty; a single light burned at the far end.

"That's his room," Angela whispered. "We go this way."

She led him down a dark passage which smelled of musty wood and dank stone. They came to the steps, cut of limestone. The centers were worn into scoops after centuries of use. Ross nearly slipped.

"Careful," she whispered. "Better turn on the light."

Ross clicked on the pencil beam. It gave sufficient illumination to get them down to the floor below. They faced a second hall, on the ground floor. Ross raised his beam and swung it around. He paused at the stuffed head of a wild boar.

"Very lifelike."

"Sssshhhh."

He turned off the light. Angela seemed to know exactly where they were going. They followed the hallway to the end, feeling their way in the darkness, touching the stone. There, they paused and waited, listening to the sound of their own tense breathing. They heard nothing. Ross was about to move forward, but Angela held him back.

"Wait," she hissed.

He waited, and then he heard. It was low, the sound of a man humming. They listened, until they were sure it was approaching them. They moved back as they saw the first glimmer of light in the adjoining hallway.

"Must be Joaquim," Angela whispered.

They stepped back, moving into a doorway, out of sight. The light came closer; the humming became louder. It was tuneless, mindless, relaxed. They saw the light; it moved, a hand lantern, swinging loosely.

Closer.

Ross sucked in his breath.

Still closer.

Now the hallway was brightly lit by the swinging lantern, and they could hear footsteps. The humming grew still louder.

Then Joaquim passed, his massive shadow trailing behind him. He continued down the hallway, past them.

Ross gave a slow sigh.

"Close," Angela whispered. "Wait."

They remained crouched in the shadows of the doorway for five minutes, and then they heard Joaquim return. Apparently, he was making the late rounds. Ross waited until he had passed a second time, still humming, still casting a massive shadow, then he moved out.

"No. Wait."

Ten more minutes passed. Nothing happened. Finally, Angela stepped out of the doorway.

"Let's go."

They headed down the hallway, silently, their feet quiet on the stone floors. Angela ducked to the right, and Ross followed. They entered a black room of great dimensions. He could tell that by listening to her voice.

"The kitchen," she whispered. "They keep the keys on the far wall, on a board. Wait here."

"Want my light?"

"No," she whispered, and moved off.

"Be careful."

She seemed to know her way around; after a few moments, she whispered, "Okay, I have them. Come over here. But be careful—there's a table in the middle of the room."

"Can't I use my light?"

"No. Windows."

Ross moved forward in the darkness, gingerly. He kept his

hands in front of him. He had no idea where the table was; he had never been in the kitchen before. He moved forward carefully, feeling each step.

Then it happened.

He struck the table with full force. It was lower than the level of his hands, and he caught it at the waist. There was a loud clattering of pots and pans.

Outside, the dog barked angrily.

"Now you've done it!"

"Sorry."

"Come on! We've got to get out of here. Let's move."

He flicked on his light. He heard running feet inside the house, heavy feet.

Outside, the Doberman was still barking.

"We've got to run for it," Angela said. She threw open the door. He saw the lawn, the fountain—now quiet— and the red Mercedes in the driveway.

"Where's the garage?"

"Over there."

She was running. He followed. The dog barked, some-where in the distance. He felt the night wind and his feet crunching on the gravel drive.

In the castle, a window was flung open, spilling light out-side. A voice said, "Who's there?"

They ran.

It seemed miles to the garage. It took hours to get there. Ross was panting, gasping for breath. The gravel of the drive seemed to suck at his shoes, holding him back, making him slip. He fell once, the hard stones striking his face. He scram-bled to his feet as the sound of the dog grew louder in his ears.

"Come on, come on," Angela said.

He reached the garage. The Porsche was there, the top

down. She jumped in behind the wheel and flicked on the lights. He got in beside her, and as he did, he saw a hammer and screwdriver on the concrete beside the car.

Oh, Christ, he thought, they've jimmied the car.

Then the ignition caught, the motor roared to life, and she started to put it in gear. Ross grabbed the hammer, slammed the door shut, and she roared down the drive.

The dog came up, with lightning speed, its jaws wide.

Before Ross could do anything, it had fixed on his hand, sinking the teeth deep. Angela shifted to second. The car gained speed, but the dog kept pace, holding firm.

With a vicious swing, Ross brought the hammer down on the dog's head, striking between the ears. The dog shuddered, gripped tighter, and held on.

He swung again, and heard bone crunch. The dog gave a moan, went limp, and released its grip.

The wind was tugging at his hair. He pulled his hand back in; it was bleeding.

"You all right?"

"Yeah, fine."

"What happened to the dog?"

"Dead, I hope."

He tore his shirt and wrapped it around his hand. The punctures were deep, and it hurt.

"I think we're going to make it," Angela said.

She increased speed. They roared off, toward the gate.

The count was screaming, hopping up and down. "Are they going? Are they going?"

Joaquim ran up and picked up the count, scooping him up bodily, holding him in the crook of his arm.

"Yes, sir. They're going."

From his vantage point, the count squinted, watching the receding red lights of the Porsche.

"They are. Do you think we frightened them?"

"I think so, sir."

"Good," the count said. He watched, cradled like a small child watching a parade, until the car was gone. Then he shook himself impatiently.

"Put me down," he said.

The count and Joaquim, looking like father and son, walked down the drive toward the fallen body of the dog. They stopped and stood over it for a moment. Then the count bent over and touched the dog's head. He removed his fingers and felt the blood.

"Poor Franco."

"Yes."

"Still, I suppose it was worth it."

"Yes, sir."

The count lifted up the lifeless head, looked at it, touching the jaws, the sharp teeth.

"He was a good dog," he said. "Kill them both as soon as you know the truth."

Joaquim nodded solemnly.

They went back inside.

17. GRANADA

"Where now?" Ross said.

They had passed the gates of the castle and were moving swiftly down the road, toward the city of Granada, brightly lit, stretching across the plain below. The night was cool.

"Anywhere you say."

"A motel?"

"I don't think we dare," she said.

"We have to stay nearby," Ross said.

"Why?"

"Tell you later." He bent over and turned on the map light beneath the dashboard. He checked his hand quickly, examining the wound.

"How is it?" Angela said.

"Not good."

"There's a doctor I know," she said, "in town."

"Can we trust him?"

"Probably. He works for the British consulate."

Ross flexed his fingers, which had already begun to swell.

"Okay," he said, "let's go see him."

They drove into town, and Angela parked before a modest house in the west end. When the doctor answered the door in his pajamas, he was in a bad mood, but he agreed to treat Ross.

"Nasty," the doctor said, holding the hand in the light in his office. "Very nasty. Wolf?"

"Just a dog," Ross said. "Damnedest thing, we were just walking down the street back to our car, and a lady was walking her dog, and all of a sudden—"

"What kind of dog?" the doctor said, swabbing with alcohol. Ross winced. "Sorry," he said.

"A cocker spaniel," Ross said. "It looked like."

"Nasty bites, for a cocker," the doctor said. "I had a cocker once. He didn't bite like this, I can tell you." He continued swabbing.

"Well, it looked like a cocker."

"You'll want to report this to the health authorities, of course."

Ross looked at Angela. "Of course."

"As soon as I'm through, I'll call—"

"It's rather late," Angela said. "Could we do it in the morning?"

"We shouldn't really," the doctor said.

"She was a sweet old lady," Ross said. "She was awfully apologetic. A Mrs. McPherson."

"McPherson? Then she was English?"

"Oh yes," Ross said. "She's calling our hotel in the morning. Going to have the dog checked first thing."

"Ah," the doctor said. "Well then."

The doctor bandaged the hand carefully, then leaned back. "Have you had a tetanus shot?"

Ross looked puzzled.

"That's the shot to prevent lockjaw," the doctor explained. "Most travelers get a booster."

Ross thought, half a cubic centimeter of antitoxin. "I'm not sure," he said. "I had so many shots, it's hard to keep track…"

"I'll just give you another," the doctor said. He filled a syringe. "What sort of work do you do, Mr. Ross?"

"I'm an insurance adjuster," Ross said, and made a face as the needle jabbed in.

❊

They left the doctor after promising to call back in the morning. Angela drove away, out of the town.

"We can go south," she said, "to the coast. And catch a boat—"

"No," Ross said. "We have to stay nearby."

"But why?"

"Because," Ross said, "it's here."

"The emerald?"

He nodded.

"But where? How do you know?"

Ross sighed. "I wasn't sure, until just an hour ago. Then I made the connection. Hamid. He had been hired by the count to steal the body and bring it down here. But he didn't deliver."

"I know," Angela said, "but I don't see how that explains anything."

"Hamid," Ross said. "It's an Arab name, not a Spanish name."

"So?"

"Think," Ross said. "Where would you hide the most valuable single jewel in the world if you were a Spanish Arab?"

She smiled. "An Arab would give it to his father, or his brother, or his uncle…"

"Right."

She frowned. "I still don't—"

"Hamid mentioned something to me about Washington Irving, and something about lions. I didn't understand. But now I do. Hamid took that body, with the emerald, to the logical place for any Arab to take a valuable object."

"The *Alhambra*?"

"Yes," Ross said.

"I don't believe it. The Alhambra is a park. It's got cops, and guards, and everything. How could he have gotten a body in there and hidden it?"

"The same way we're going to get it out," Ross said. "Now drive into the mountains, and let's get some sleep."

She drove high into the hills east of the town, until they were up where it was cool. She pulled off the road into a grove of olive trees. Ross sat back in his seat, sighed, and closed his eyes. Angela rested her head on his shoulder. He fell asleep almost immediately.

He awoke in the morning with hot sun streaming down onto his face. Looking over, he saw Angela curled up behind the wheel, still asleep. Carefully, so as not to wake her, he got out, stretched, yawned, and walked through the olive grove. The air was slightly damp, fresh, and clear, smelling of animals, plants, and the desert. Off to the right, a small herd of sheep grazed on the grass beneath the olive trees.

He walked until he came to a short rise and could look down on the city of Granada. Though large, and in some districts modern, it still bore the Moorish influence, with the cramped streets, the brown tile roofs and whitewashed walls, and the open courtyards. It was very beautiful in the morning light.

He stood and looked for a long tune.

It was said that the Arabs still mourned for Granada in their evening prayers. If so, they had mourned a long time; Granada fell to Ferdinand and Isabella in January, 1492, the same year the Genoese lunatic, Columbus, discovered America. Granada, until then, represented the last and strongest foothold of the Arabs in Europe. It was easy to see why— rising high above the town, on a sharp, steep series of hills, was the Alhambra, the complex of palaces and fortresses which had housed the Moorish kings, their nobles, and harems for hundreds of years. The name, literally, meant purple-red, which was the color of the buildings. On an adjoining hill was the Generalife, the summer residence of the Moorish court, composed of white, pristine buildings.

And everywhere were gardens, trees, fountains, running water…an exotic fortress of great beauty and craftsmanship. The hills were covered with trees and the palaces decked with flowers; the temperature there was ten to twenty degrees lower than the one-hundred-degree heat of the desert and the city of Granada on the plains. In Granada, the heat, the dust, and the burning light were brilliantly hot; in the Alhambra, everything was cool, verdant, and sensual.

Now, in the twentieth century, it was difficult to imagine the caliphs, the harems, the eunuchs, the sorcerers and alchemists and noblemen who had lived on that mountaintop. Below, in the city, were the spires of a Catholic cathedral and the modern buildings of a bank, a hotel, a garage. Yet the mountain retained a sense of mystery, of greenery and seclusion, of secret sensuality, even from afar.

"What are you thinking about?" He looked over; Angela was there.

"Dancing girls," he said, "in the moonlight."

"The Alhambra?"

He nodded.

"Are you sure about it?"

"As sure as I can be."

"And you know how to get in?"

He smiled. "For the moment," he said, "we simply pay the tourist entrance fee and walk in."

"As simple as that?"

"Let's hope so." He smiled. "Come on. Let's go: we've got to stop in town."

"What for?"

"Sandwiches and a bottle of wine."

"Why?"

"You'll see."

As they drove down in the Porsche, Ross found himself frowning. Angela said, "Something the matter?"

"I keep thinking about Joaquim. Did you notice his hands?"

"They're huge. Immense."

"No, I meant the scars. He had some peculiar hook-shaped scars that were obviously very deep."

She shrugged. "Perhaps he got them in a fight."

"No," Ross said. "I don't think so. Something else."

"What?"

"I don't know. But I keep wondering whether those scars came from the same knife that was used on Carrini and his men and on Hamid."

"You think Joaquim killed them?"

"No. He's strong, and he's powerful, but he could never kill Carrini and his three friends. Not all together, in a group. Not without help."

"Maybe he had help."

"Yes," Ross said. "That's what I'm afraid of."

18. ISMAEL

Joaquim stood in the center of the courtyard at the far side of the castle. He stood very straight, his huge body clothed in stiff cloth fabric, his face covered with a wire mask rather like a dueling mask, except that it enclosed his whole head.

In his hands, he held a rope thirty feet long. Attached to the end of the rope was a quarter pound of filet mignon. He set the meat on the stone floor of the courtyard and picked up a can of aerosol spray. He shook the can, then held it over the meat and sprayed it for several seconds. A rich, heavy odor filled the air.

From the far corner of the courtyard, the count said, "Are you ready?"

"Yes."

"Then swing it."

Joaquim lifted the rope and began to swing it in a slow circle, paying out the line as he went. Soon the beef was whistling through the air.

"Higher," said the count. "Keep it high."

The count was dressed in a Chinese bathrobe of red silk. His feet were bare, and he moved cautiously across the courtyard. He stopped beside a low building and pulled on a stiff leather glove. He flexed his fingers, then stepped back.

"I'm going to use Ismael today," the count said. "He is the most ruthless. Be careful."

"I will," Joaquim said.

The count nodded and pulled on a wire helmet similar to

the one worn by Joaquim. Then he opened a door and stepped into a low building.

A soft fluttering sound greeted him.

"Hello, my pretties. Anyone hungry?" He scanned the rows of perched birds. There were six, each trained to varying degrees. They regarded him gravely, with unblinking eyes. Their long beaks, curved at the end, were sharp and businesslike.

The finest falcons money could buy. He smiled to himself. Ross and the girl would be so surprised. They were fools, of course, not to have suspected: it had been a tradition in Granada for generations. At one time, a whole quarter in the city had been given over to the falcon trainers. Now, it was the province of noblemen, men with the time and money to engage in the expensive, slow, dangerous process of training a bird of prey.

"Ismael," the count said. "How are you today?"

Ismael cocked his head. He was a large, fierce bird, weighing twenty pounds, all muscle and tearing beak, nothing wasted, no fat.

"You want to play a game?"

The count held up his gloved hand, moving slowly so as not to frighten the bird. Ismael hesitated, then stepped onto the outstretched finger. The count felt the sharp talons grip the glove in a fierce hold.

"Good, my pretty. Very good."

Again, with a slow gesture, he raised the leather hood with his free hand and placed it over the falcon's head. Ismael gave a little wriggle as the hood was set in place. Then he relaxed.

The count stroked the smooth feathers.

"Very good, very good."

He took the bird outside.

Of all the birds, Ismael was his favorite. He had named it after determining that it had great intelligence, yet a vicious ruthlessness which surpassed all caution. It was almost human, this falcon: it became so caught up in the vigor of its attack, it became foolhardy, mindlessly brave.

Yet effective. Undeniably effective.

The falcon could do anything. He had seen Ismael attack and kill a two-year-old bull. The bird had struck three times, first at the eyes, then at the neck, and finally, slashing with the beak until the animal bled to death. Twenty pounds of fighting flesh killing two hundred pounds.

"We have work for you, Ismael," the count said, stroking the feathers soothingly.

In the courtyard, Joaquim was swinging the meat. He was making high circles, the beef still whistling as it made its arc.

"Are you ready?"

"Ready," Joaquim said.

Joaquim was used to this. He had been attacked many times by young falcons in the early stages of training. So, for that matter, had the count, though expensive plastic surgery had covered all traces. "All right, my pretty."

He removed the leather hood and gave a shake of his gloved hand. The falcon flew up, its head twisting jerkily as it climbed. It went up and up, more than a thousand feet into the air, and then began circling. From the ground, the count thought it hardly possible that the falcon could see, but he knew better.

Ismael circled. A minute passed, then two. The falcon went wide, over the town of Granada, spreading its wings and gliding effortlessly. Then it returned. Joaquim still swung the beef. This was how they had trained the falcons, and this was how they had learned the truth about falcons' sense of smell. The experts said that falcons hunted by sight alone and could smell nothing. The count knew better. From long experience. A falcon could be trained to hunt by smell, and to hunt with murderous success.

"Coming back," the count said.

High above, almost lost in the hot Andalusian sun, Ismael circled. It moved without exertion, its wings spread, floating on the high currents. Then it happened.

The count had seen it before, but each time it gave him a fresh thrill. Ismael pulled in its wings, folding tightly into a black muscular knot, and fell like a stone. It dropped, gathering speed, moving thirty, then sixty, then one hundred miles an hour. It was screaming through the air, beak forward, talons spread, ready to rip and tear...

It hit the meat.

With an animal scream, Ismael gripped the filet, grabbed it, yanked, and pulled it free of the rope. It climbed twenty feet, tearing the meat, pecking at it, and then released it. The meat fell and landed in a small cloud of dust in the courtyard. Ismael climbed higher again, circled once more, and then descended slowly to the count's outstretched, gloved hand. It gripped the finger, flapped its wings a final time, beating a wind around the count's face. Then it was quiet. "Good bird, very good," the count said. He slipped on the hood.

The bird was trained, of course, to attack the scented meat so long as it moved. When it was still, it did not attack.

"I think Ismael will do marvelously," the count said. "Just marvelously."

"You will spray those two?"

"Yes," the count said. "And the professor as well."

"Are you certain he is here?"

"Oh, absolutely," the count said. He gave a small, childish laugh and returned the falcon to the roost.

The girl was waiting in the count's study. "Well," the count said, "are you ready?"

"Yes," she said.

"Here is the spray," he said, handing her the aerosol. "Pretend it is insecticide."

She nodded.

"But before you go, dye your hair. Ross will remember you."

She gave a short laugh. "He won't remember me. He was so frightened of the cops, he won't remember a thing. And I gave him some song and dance—"

"Dye your hair," the count said. "Dye it black. And fix the makeup on your eyes."

Subdued, she said, "Yes, sir."

"Now remember. There will be five. Ross, a girl, the professor, another man, and another girl. You must spray all five. Understood?"

"Understood."

19. THE ALHAMBRA

They bought coarse bread, salami, and cheese in a little store downtown; also a bottle of wine. As Angela made sandwiches, she said, "I really don't understand this. There are restaurants within the Alhambra, you know."

"I know. But they won't be open at night."

"We're staying up there?"

"Yes. After it closes."

"And search?"

"That's right," Ross said.

They got into the car and drove through the town until they reached the base of the mountain on which the Alhambra was perched. A road led up through green forested parks.

"We'll leave the car here," he said. "Out of sight."

They began the long walk up the mountain, keeping to the side of the road, letting tourist cars and buses pass.

"There will be thousands up there today," Angela said, watching the cars.

"So much the better. The crowds will help us."

As they climbed, the air became cooler and quieter; the noisy bustle of the city was left below, with the heat and shimmering light. Along the road, in an ancient cut stone trough, water gurgled. The system of irrigation which supported the lush growth on the mountain was a marvel.

"I like it here," she said.

"It will be cold at night. We should have brought sweaters."

"Do you think it will take long? To find the body, I mean."

"No, not long."

"Do you think the count has started to search for us?"

"I'm sure of it. But not here—he'll be looking in Madrid, or Barcelona. Anywhere but right here, under his nose."

"Sooner or later, he'll figure it out."

"That's true," Ross said. "And he'll come after us."

"What will we do then?"

"Run like hell," Ross said, "and hope for the best."

"If he catches us, he'll kill us," Angela said. "I know it."

"No," Ross said. "He won't."

"How do you know?"

"Because we'll have hidden the emerald. It's our ace in the hole."

"I hope you're right."

"So do I."

Angela shuddered. They said nothing more until they reached the top and entered through the ancient, elaborately decorated horseshoe gates of the palace. Just inside, the tour buses were parked, and groups of tourists were forming around shouting guides. Along one wall, a row of vendors sold trinkets, souvenirs, and guidebooks. All around, magnificent, red-brown, stood the buildings and palaces. Directly in front of them was the square palace of Carlos V. Behind that were the old Arab gardens and palaces. To the east, occupying a corner of the mountain, was the fortress, the Alcazaba.

They paused to buy a map from one of the squatting vendors. Ross noticed that among all the guidebooks were copies of Washington Irving's *Legends of the Alhambra*.

He remembered the dying words of Hamid: "Twenty paces east from Washington Irving…"

Did he mean here?

Ross turned to Angela. "Which way is east?"

"I don't know. Check the map."

He did. East took them toward the Alcazaba. He casually stepped off twenty paces and found himself in the middle of a small garden, halfway between the palace of Carlos and the fortress. There were dozens of tourists everywhere, all around.

He walked back to Angela.

"Something wrong?"

"No. Just a little confused."

"You get the wrong directions?"

He scratched his head. "Maybe. Or maybe I heard wrong…"

Twenty paces. He tried to recall the conversation exactly. Hamid's words had been tense, the last gasps of a dying man. Was it twenty paces?

He tried thirty, then forty. Nothing; he was still left standing in the middle of the garden. He switched directions, going north instead of east, but found nothing. One or two tourists, watching him, were beginning to mutter among themselves; he decided to stop.

"We need a guidebook," Ross said.

Angela bought one, and he thumbed to the index, looking under Irving, Washington. He found the proper page.

There was only a paragraph, describing the American writer's fascination with the hilltop fortress and his careful collection of all fables associated with the buildings. Several of the stories were summarized at the bottom of the page. Ross glanced over them briefly.

Then, returning to the text, he read: "A bronze plaque, 16 by 24 inches, stands in the south wall of the Palacio Arabe, commemorating Washington Irving's interest in the Alhambra. It was erected in 1894, and bears the inscription…"

"Come on," Ross said, closing the book. "I think I know…"

"Worked it out?"

They walked across the courtyard, toward the Arab Palaces.

"I had the number of paces right. But I was starting from the wrong place."

They came up to the plaque, the letters raised and slightly corroded.

"Washington Irving," Ross said. "Twenty paces east from the Washington Irving…"

He stepped it off. He was heading for the Alcazaba, with its twenty-foot-high walls of brown masonry. He covered fourteen paces, then sixteen, and stopped.

At sixteen, he was up against the wall.

"Wrong again," Angela said.

"Maybe my paces were too big. Hamid was shorter."

Angela lit a cigarette, and Ross leaned against the wall. He thought about the problem. Even if he reduced the size of his steps, he would strike the wall too early. That couldn't be it.

He looked around the ground, but the dirt was hard-packed, undisturbed.

"Maybe it's inside the wall itself," Angela said. "Maybe there's a secret tunnel or a passage."

They turned to look at the wall, running their fingers over the crude bricks, touching, feeling.

"Señor y Señorita."

They turned. It was a policeman. He looked at them curiously.

"Yes?" Ross said.

"A pleasant day," the policeman said, touching his cap. But the eyes were alert and watchful.

"Yes," Ross said. "We were just admiring the masonry. The ancient methods were excellent."

The policeman's face showed hesitation, then relief. They were tourists examining the masonry, touching it. Nothing more complicated. He smiled. "Indeed, we are very proud of it."

He touched his cap again and moved off.

Angela sucked on her cigarette and watched him leave. "I was frozen up," she said. "I wanted to say something, but I couldn't. I just froze."

"It's all right," Ross said. "It doesn't matter."

He snapped his fingers, and shook his head.

"Of course," he said. "Twenty paces. That's *inside* the wall."

"You mean inside the fortress itself?"

"Yes. It can't be anything else."

They hurried inside the fortress, passing through the arched, carved gate and climbing a ramp that led to a parapet. There, they could look down over the interior of the fort. For the most part, it was old and uninteresting—utilitarian barracks, squat buildings, and heavy stonework.

Ross saw that a section of the fort had collapsed and was under repair. It was fenced off from the public, with signs in four languages to keep away.

"What's underneath the fort?"

"A cellar, I think. For storing ammunition and supplies."

"That's it," Ross said. "I'm sure of it."

"Sure of what?"

"Where the body is."

"What do we do?" she said.

"We check. I check."

"And what am I supposed to do?"

"Stand guard."

They climbed down from the parapet and walked across the courtyard of the fort to the place where the floor had collapsed, opening onto the cellars beneath. They looked down the hole. A musty, dank odor rose into the sunlight.

"Lovely," Angela said.

Ross turned and glanced around the courtyard. A group of tourists were lined up at a far corner, waiting to climb up a round tower. Nobody was paying them much attention. He gave her the guidebook.

"Here. You can pretend to read this."

"What are you doing?"

"Going down there."

"You're crazy."

"Probably." He grinned and slipped under the fence. "See you."

It was a drop of ten feet to the stone floor below. He poised on the edge, tensed himself, and jumped. He landed on all fours, raising a cloud of dust.

"You all right?" Angela said.

"Fine."

He looked around. A series of arched rooms and tunnels led off, fading into darkness. There was a smell of decay, damp stone, and ancient dust. He sneezed, hearing the sound echo through the vaults. He paused to get his bearings, then headed off in what he hoped was the right direction.

As he left the hole, it became shadowy, then completely dark. Fortunately, he still had his penlight; he clicked it on. The batteries were already weakening, the light turning yellow. He would have to be careful; the light was helpful now, but it would be essential when he returned in the evening.

He passed through a room which had obviously been a dungeon. There were small cramped cubicles and heavy rusted bars. Iron rings on the walls once held torches; he could see spots of lampblack on the ceiling. On the floor, the dust was several inches deep; probably no one had set foot here for centuries.

Or had they?

He looked and saw the clear imprint of a man's foot. Then another, and another. They were leading west, toward the wall. He noticed the pattern, the unevenness of the steps.

Like a man staggering under a heavy weight.

Hamid.

With the body.

He followed the impressions through the dust. Around him, everything was black. All he could see was the small cone of yellow light coming from his penlight.

He moved forward.

The air became colder and damper. And he began to hear sounds. At first, it was a clicking, very far off. As he approached, it became a chattering, like the excited jabber of monkeys. The odor in the passage became more fetid, and it turned still colder.

The noise was louder.

What was it?

Abruptly, the passage took a sharp right-angle turn, and he saw. The body, still draped in white, lay in a corner.

And he also saw the source of the chattering.

Rats.

20. THE ODDS FAVORED IT

He stood for a moment in horror. There were hundreds of them, some more than a foot long. They crawled over the body in a thick swarm, chattering, shoving, gnawing at the cloth. In places, they had torn through and were at the flesh of the body.

The smell here was very bad. He looked at the rats, and in his flashlight, they turned glowing beady eyes on him. He shifted the light away and fought a moment of nausea. He leaned against the wall, feeling damp stone, breathed deeply, and turned away, stumbling, heading back to the hole, to daylight, to the sun and the air.

Behind him, he heard the infernal chattering.

He tripped, almost fell, and caught himself. He was moving quickly, as quickly as he could. Up ahead, he saw sunlight filtering down through the dust.

The hole. Thank God.

He reached it and looked up, blinking in the bright light.

"Angela?"

"Yes."

"Is it all right? Can I come up?"

"Yes, but quickly."

A heap of rubble stood near one side of the hole. He scrambled up, reached the lip, and came over. It took just a moment to slip out through the fence and join her.

"Did you find it?"

"Yes."

"Intact?"

"I couldn't tell," Ross said. "The rats beat me to it."

Angela wrinkled her nose. "There are rats up here, too. Someone's been watching us."

"Where?"

She nodded vaguely toward the parapet, not pointing. "A man. Up there. He left as you started to come up."

"What did he look like?"

"He was very fat and pale. I couldn't see much more. He had sunglasses."

"The professor," Ross said.

"Who is he?"

"Damned if I know."

"Is he after the emerald too?"

"Isn't everyone?" Ross said. He squinted up at the parapet. "Well, anyway. Now he knows."

"Do you think he'll try to get it?"

"If he does, he's in for a surprise. You can't get near that body with less than a small army. The rats are all over the place."

"Then how are we going to do it?"

Ross shook his head. "I don't know."

They left the fort and wandered over toward the Arab Palaces.

"Where now?"

"Let's walk through the grounds. I need time to think, and I'm not quite ready for lunch."

They walked, marveling at the beauty of the place. The palaces were a series of open courts, with ponds, gurgling water, splashing fountains, and greenery. The buildings were graceful, beautifully decorated in limestone and carved stone, intensely, richly decorated.

As they walked, Ross said, "You know, Hamid said something very odd."

"What's that?"

"He talked about another place, about lions. Down low, by the lions, near the water. And he said one was real, and the other not…"

"What does it mean?"

"Damned if I know." He reached for the map. "There's a place here called Patio de los Leones. That's the Court of Lions."

"Yes. It's very famous. But we haven't come there yet."

Ten minutes later, passing through cool secluded gardens and sparkling fountains, they arrived. The Court of Lions was rectangular and open to the sun. In the center was a large circular basin and fountain, supported by twelve stone bodies of lions, each spouting water through its mouth. Leading down to the central fountain were four small rivulets of water, coming from the four sides of the court.

"So this is it," Ross said.

"And Hamid said?"

"Down low, near the water."

They headed for the central fountain, just as a party of fifty tourists arrived, swarming around the court, while the guide shouted names, dates, and facts. The tourists scratched themselves, took photographs, and sipped the water. Nobody paid any attention to the guide.

Ross stopped. "We can't search now. We'll have to wait."

"What do you expect to find?"

"I don't know."

They turned away, moving through still other gardens. It was now almost noon, and they were both hungry. They headed for a restaurant, located at one corner of the mountaintop. On the way, a voice called,

"Oh, Doctor."

Ross stopped and turned. Puffing slightly, the professor came up to them.

"I thought I'd find you eventually."

"Yes," Ross said.

"Having a good time?" the professor asked pleasantly. He wore a lightweight blue suit, which wrinkled around his bulging abdomen. His tie was a map of the world: Mercator projection.

"Fine, thanks."

"And Miss Angela Locke. How are you today?"

Ross started. "You know her?"

"In a way. I know she works for the count."

"Did," Angela corrected.

"Oh, there's been a falling out, has there? I'm not surprised. The odds favored it. And what are you two young people doing now?"

"Sightseeing," Ross said. "Pure and simple."

"Wonderful, wonderful I'm pleased for both of you. You must allow me to take you to lunch."

"Thanks anyway, but—"

"I insist," the professor said.

"Really quite impossible."

The professor grinned. "A clash of wills," he said. "How quaint. Would it change your mind if I told you I had a gun in my pocket?"

"It might," Ross said.

"Please do reconsider," the professor said. "Besides, I would like you to meet a friend."

"Your flighty assistant?"

"Please," the professor said. "Jackman would be terribly hurt if he heard you talk that way."

Ross sighed.

They went into the restaurant. It was pleasant, with an open court, palm trees, flowering geraniums and orchids. Sitting at a far table, Ross saw a blonde woman; her back was to them. But as they approached, Ross began to have a strange feeling...

"I think you've met her," the professor said. "Miss Brenner, my special assistant."

Karin turned and smiled. "Dr. Ross."

"Well well," Ross said. "Well, well, well."

They all sat down. The professor introduced Angela, then said, "Now then: shall we order?"

Neither Ross nor Angela said much during the meal. Ross thought of several nasty things to say to Karin, but he knew she wouldn't care what he said, and besides, it was too late now.

Toward the end of the meal, the professor said, "I must admit that I underestimated you, Doctor. I thought you were naïve and innocent. I must revise my opinion."

"Just lucky," Ross said.

"I think not. Your chances of getting so far are infinitesimally small, I assure you. You are to be congratulated."

"Is that before I'm shot, or afterward?"

"Then too," the professor said, ignoring the comment, "you have acquired a charming young lady." He smiled at Angela. "Most charming."

Angela looked away, smoking a cigarette.

"You may be wondering, Doctor," the professor continued, "why I arranged this meeting. I had no desire to upset you. Quite the contrary. I have the utmost respect for you. But I hope seeing Miss Brenner here will jolt you into an understanding of the complexities of this situation. Complexities which you barely understand."

"You're suggesting I get out."

"Before you are killed, yes."

"Who will kill me?"

"I haven't the foggiest," the professor said.

"Not you?"

"Me? How absurd. I am here on holiday. A simple holiday."

"I see."

"The Moorish influence on Spanish art and architecture has always fascinated me, you know."

"Yes. Fascinating."

"Yes," the professor said, smoothing his tie, caressing India and Africa.

"Will you stay long?" Ross said.

"Not long. You?"

"We're leaving tonight."

"Imagine. So am I."

"That's interesting," Ross said.

"Yes."

The meal was finished; they drank coffee, then the professor paid the bill. They all got up from the table and walked out the entranceway, garlanded with flowers. There, a girl in a waitress uniform was spraying the air with insect repellent. As the four of them walked past, the girl accidentally sprayed them all, catching them across the back of the neck and shoulders.

The professor spun and swore loudly in fluent Spanish. The girl dropped the can and apologized profusely, sputtering, hanging her head.

"Stupid bloody fool," the professor said, touching his damp neck. "Never teach these people anything. Damnable country." He sighed. "Oh well. At least we won't get bitten by mosquitoes today, eh?"

He laughed. Outside, in the sunlight, he extended his hand.

"Good luck, Doctor. I trust you'll have a successful career." He bowed slightly. "Miss Locke."

Ross shook hands.

"Good luck to you, Professor. I think you're in for some surprises, later." He remembered the rats, swarming, chattering, crawling...

"Oh, I think we are all in for some surprises," the professor said with an easy smile. "Good day."

Angela and Ross watched them go: the professor, trundling and fat; Karin Brenner, blonde and wholesome. They made a weird pair.

"What did you think?" Ross said.

"They're crazy," Angela said. "Both of them." She frowned and sniffed. "This insect stuff really stinks, doesn't it?"

"Yes," Ross said. "Almost like a bad cologne. I suppose we could try to wash it off."

"Why bother?"

They set off, continuing through the grounds. It was later in the day, now, and the sun was sinking, no longer so fiercely hot and bright. They moved on to the Generalife and remained there until sunset, passing through the gardens, the fountains, the cool airy rooms.

As the sky deepened, turning from blue to purple and finally violet, Ross said, "Full moon tonight."

"That's good."

"We'll need it."

"Do you think the professor will stay on the grounds?"

"I'm certain of it. What are we going to do?"

"Watch him," Ross said. "Watch him like a hawk."

Despite their best efforts, the professor and Karin eluded them late in the afternoon. Ross and Angela searched for them for another hour and then gave up. They had dinner in another restaurant, and then hid behind a hedge near the main gardens of the Alhambra. The light was failing; only a few scattered tourists remained on the grounds. A guard walked by, repeating mechanically that the Palace was closing, the Palace was closing, all visitors must now leave, all visitors must now leave…

"Does anybody stay the night?" Angela whispered.

"Don't think so. Maybe some custodians, to clean up. Maybe a few guards."

Angela scratched the back of her neck. "You know, I still smell that spray junk. I thought it would wear off, but it hasn't."

"No time to worry about it now."

An hour passed. It became quite dark. The last of the tourists and daytime guards left the park.

They were alone.

Cautiously, they stepped out of the bushes. The moon was up, bathing the grounds in silver light. It was unearthly, the silent buildings, the placid ponds, a fantasy under the light of the moon.

"Beautiful," Angela said, looking around.

"Shhhh."

He led her off, stealthily, through the buildings. They were headed back toward the Court of Lions. Ross wanted to have another look at the statues around the base.

"Where do you suppose the professor is?" Angela whispered.

They came out into the court, silent, peaceful.

"Right here," said a voice. They turned and saw a faint figure in the shadows. "And I still have my gun."

21. THE HOLE

"Well, Professor."

"Well, Doctor. We meet again, and under such auspicious circumstances. I am afraid I need your help."

"You won't get it."

"You're mistaken."

There were two whooshing, spitting sounds, and the dirt in front of Ross was kicked up in tiny chunks.

"You see, I am not joking about the gun. Nor am I joking about your help. I need it."

"What for?"

"The gas," the professor said. "You must handle the gas."

"Why don't you have one of your friends help you?"

"Because," the professor said, "they are busy with other matters. This is a complex problem; I warned you before. Besides, I knew I could count on you. Please walk off to your right, and follow the path."

He directed them through the palaces, the ghostly moonlit rooms, to a small shack in a corner of a garden. It was obviously a workman's toolshed.

"Now then. Stand back."

They did. The professor took aim and fired the gun. The lock was shattered, and the doors creaked open.

"Look inside," he said. "You will find a tank, a pair of gas masks, and several large flashlights."

Ross looked. He found everything. The tank was fitted with a harness so it could strap over your back; there was a hose leading to a nozzle, like a flamethrower.

"I suppose you had this brought in specially?"

"Heavens no. You give me too much credit. This is all the property of the Spanish government."

"Oh? What's the gas?"

"A chlorothion derivative of some sort. Nerve gas, essentially. They spray most of the buildings here once a month, during the evenings."

"For the rats?"

"Yes. A serious problem. Can't have rats showing up in Spain's largest tourist attraction, can we?"

"And you're going to use this gas underneath, in the hole?"

The professor smiled. "No," he said. "You are."

Standing in the courtyard of the fortress, staring down at the hole, he felt like a visitor from another planet. The tank was strapped on his back; he wore heavy gloves to protect his hands from the concentrated spray near the nozzle; over his face, the mask was fitted, black and snoutlike.

"Whenever you're ready," the professor said. He pulled on a second mask, and it muffled his voice. "I fear we have only two masks, so Angela will wait up here. You will go down first, Doctor. I will follow some distance behind, with an extra light, and the gun."

He turned to Angela. "I shall expect you to wait here patiently, my dear. I don't need to tell you that if we come back up and you are not here, I will shoot the good doctor. Immediately."

Angela nodded, bit her lip, said nothing.

"All right then. Let's get started. Down you go, Doctor."

Ross clambered to the edge of the hole and jumped into the darkness.

He landed, clanging the tank on the stone floor, and got up.

He switched on the electric torch; it gave a reassuringly bright light. Behind him, he heard the professor clambering down, breathing heavily through the mask, his breath hissing into the canister in front of the nosepiece.

"Lead on," the professor said, switching his own light on.

Ross set out.

In a sense, it was better at night. Wearing the mask, he smelled nothing but rubber and metal, none of the dank smells of the cellar. And at night, the darkness was somehow less terrifying. He went forward quickly and only slowed when he heard the clicking and chattering. It made his skin crawl.

"I hear it," the professor said. "Keep going."

They did, and the sounds grew louder, until finally they rounded the corner and saw the body, covered with squirming furry bodies.

"Now," said the professor, his voice tense. "Do it now!"

Ross turned on the gas.

It jetted out with a sizzling, sputtering sound, a thin white mist that ran along the floor. The rats responded instantly. The gas caught the first animals unaware, and as the vapors reached them, they went into twitching, spastic convulsions, flopping onto their backs, baring their teeth, urinating and defecating in the final moments. The other rats panicked and fled, chattering as they went.

"Spray everything. The corpse, the whole room. We don't want them back."

Ross moved forward, kicking aside the fallen bodies on the floor. He fought his nausea: Christ, it wouldn't do to vomit in the mask. He sprayed as quickly as he could, and then stepped back.

"All right," the professor said. "Good enough."

He moved forward, toward the corpse. Now Ross could

see clearly the extent of damage. In many places the shroud had been eaten away. The professor took out a knife and opened the shroud in a single smooth movement. The body was not pretty, and he turned aside for a moment before continuing.

Ross moved closer and concentrated on the incision he had made several days before. But before he had a good look, the professor had sliced down the sutures and peeled back the skin to expose the heart.

"Ah."

His hands reached forward and came up with the box. It was the same one Ross had originally inserted.

"At last," the professor said. He held the box in his hand, feeling its weight. "At last."

He motioned to Ross. "We can leave now. After you, Doctor."

Ross looked back at the body. "You're leaving now? Like this?"

"Exactly."

"It's—"

"*Now*, Doctor." He wagged the gun.

Ross walked back toward the entrance to the hole. The professor, with the gun, followed behind. A few minutes later, they scrambled up to the surface. Angela was there, her back turned to him.

The professor pulled off his mask and said, "You can take all that off now."

Ross removed his mask but left the tank on. He turned to Angela. "You all right?"

"Yes," she said, softly.

"Sure?"

"Yes," she said again, rather nervously, he thought. She didn't seem herself. Spooked, preoccupied, looking around nervously, turned away from him. Almost as if she expected something to happen.

"Did you hear something?" Ross whispered. By now, he was looking around, too. The square was brightly lit; the moon overhead was round and full. Suddenly, a dark shadow passed over them.

"What was that?"

The professor looked up irritably. "Just some bird, I expect."

Ross looked up and saw it, slowly circling in the sky.

"Damned big bird," he said.

"Never mind," the professor said. He looked at the box and sighed with evident pleasure. "I cannot tell you how I feel at this moment. And since you've both gone to so much trouble, I suppose it's only fair I give you a look."

He placed the package on the ground. He removed the cloth and exposed a metal box. There was a small hinged lid.

"Well now," he said. In the torchlight, his fingers trembled. "Here we go."

He lifted the lid. For a moment, all they saw was white cotton. The professor removed this, exposing the green peak of a stone.

"That's it," the professor said, sucking in his breath. He removed the rest of the cotton packing and lifted the emerald from the metal box.

It was huge, larger than a softball. It gleamed in the torchlight, reflecting its colors. The professor held it delicately.

"The Emerald of Cortez," he said. "At last."

And then he frowned.

"Just a minute," he said. "Just a minute, just a minute…"

He peered closely at the stone.

"Something wrong?"

"Shut up."

He turned the stone in his hand, very slowly, staring at it. Then he set it on the ground.

"Son of a bitch!" he said.

He raised his heavy torch and swung it down hard on the pyramid. There was a shattering crunch as it struck.

"Hey! What're you doing?"

The professor stepped back and shone his light down on the splintered fragments.

"Just as I thought," he said. "Glass. A glass pyramid."

22. HUNTING

For a long time, they stood in silence, looking at each other. The professor was furious, muttering and stomping in his rage. Ross glanced at Angela, who was still glancing around, then up at the sky.

"That bird's still up there," he said to her. She didn't answer.

"Damn the bird!" the professor snorted. "I want the emerald!"

Ross shrugged. "How do you propose to get it?"

"Somebody," the professor said darkly, "made a switch. I want to know who."

"I don't have any idea," Ross said. But he was thinking of Hamid and what he had said about one being real and the other false, one by the Washington Irving and the other by the lions. Hamid must have made a switch.

"You are a wretched liar," the professor said. "I believe you know exactly what I want to know. And I intend that you shall tell me."

His voice was tight. He stepped forward with the gun.

And then it happened.

Something struck Ross from behind, clanging hard against the metal gas tank. He was knocked to the ground and felt beating wings near his face, then nothing. He rolled over.

"What was that?" Ross said.

"*The bird*," the professor said in an awed voice. He was looking up. So was Angela, her pretty face turned to the sky.

Ross picked himself up. "A bird did that?"

"*That* bird did," the professor said.

They watched it wheel effortlessly in the sky, circling high above them.

"What is it?"

"A falcon. A trained falcon."

Suddenly, the bird closed its wings and began to dive.

"Run!" the professor shouted. Ross grabbed Angela's hand, and they sprinted away. The professor followed, but the bird struck him on the back, and he fell, fighting, flailing his arms.

Ross ran with Angela. He ran for everything he was worth. She let go of his hand and ran alongside him, surprising him by her ability to keep pace. Looking back, he saw the professor getting slowly to his feet as the falcon climbed skyward for another dive.

They ran out of the fortress, into a different courtyard, shaded and protected by trees. Ross stopped and leaned against a trunk, gasping for breath, his chest tight with exertion and fear.

"It's okay," he said. "We'll be safe here, for a while."

He turned to Angela.

She was not there.

"Angela?"

Silence. Nothing but the sound of a light wind in the trees.

"Angela!"

There was no answer. He was alone. Panic seized him. He ran back, retracing his steps, leaving the protected cover of the trees, returning to the fortress steps.

He was sweating now, hot and damp, and the sticky-sweet odor of the insecticide was strong in his nostrils. It was an odd smell for an insecticide, he thought. Odd and somehow familiar.

Above, wheeling, he saw the bird.

It circled over him, and he ducked into the shadows. For

a moment, it seemed to linger over his head, and then it moved away.

He looked back at the steps, and the fortress.

No one there, not even the professor.

Separated finally from Ross, Angela had run alone to a deserted part of the Arab Palace, some distance from the fortress. Leaning against the wall, gasping for breath, now reaching under the skirt to remove a small walkie talkie. Pulling out the antenna, flicking it on.

"Professor. Are you there?"

A crackling and a buzz.

"Professor? Answer me."

Finally, a tired, winded voice. "Yes, my dear. I'm here. Are you all right?"

"So far. I've lost Ross. Where are you?"

"Still in the fortress. The bird has me pinned down. And I can't move my arm. Bleeding."

"Can you shoot it?"

"No. Moves too fast." There was a moment of heavy breathing. "Much too fast. But I'll try to get to you. Did Ross tell you anything?"

"No. Nothing."

"All right. I'll try to get there. Where are you?"

She looked around, at the court, the curved arches, the serene porticoes. And above, at the sky. The bird could not be seen.

"I don't know. A court of some kind."

"Describe it."

The description was given quickly. The professor seemed to recognize it. "I'll be there as soon…as I can."

The intercom went dead. She telescoped the antenna and replaced it. Then she waited. The minutes ticked by, silent.

Finally she heard footsteps. She dropped back into the shadows, tense, thinking it might be Ross.

It was not. It was the professor, walking stooped, dangling one limp, lifeless arm. He was bleeding from a severe cut on his shoulder.

"A fiend, an absolute fiend. Where's the doctor?"

"Don't know."

"I hope to hell the falcon gets him."

"So do I."

The professor put his good arm over her shoulder and leaned on her. "You're a love. Help me a while. I know a place to hide that's better than this."

They walked for several minutes in silence, moving slowly through the rooms, the small gardens, the gurgling moonlit fountains. Once, far off, they heard a voice cry, "Angela! Angela!"

The professor chuckled. "Poor bastard."

"The falcon will get him." The voice was hoarse, angry.

They came at last to a broad courtyard with a long pool. In the moonlight, the columns were reflected in the water.

The scene was serene, peaceful. The professor stood by the edge of the pool. Blood dripped down from his arm.

"We should be safe here, for a while," he said.

Angela let him go reluctantly. "You all right?"

"Yes, yes. I'll manage."

Looking up, she saw the bird circling overhead. The professor saw it, too, reflected in the still pool. But it was too late.

Before either of them could speak, the bird had dived, struck the professor on the neck, and slashed him, shaken him, and dropped him.

He pitched forward, face down, into the pool, and lay there, swaying gently.

Angela sobbed and dropped back into the shadows.

❀

For Ross, everything had become a nightmare. He wandered frantic through the ghostly buildings, intensely beautiful in the moonlight. Yet he was lost, hopelessly lost. And Angela was gone. He thought of her, the gentle face, the soft skin—and he thought of the bird, plunging relentlessly out of the sky, talons spread, beak forward, ready to pierce and tear…

He called to her. He called until his voice was hoarse, but had no response. He continued to run aimlessly through the courts, gardens, and buildings.

Twice, the falcon came after him. The first time he was lucky, dropping into a crevice which the bird could not enter. It flapped and screamed above him, then lifted off again. He did not see it for several minutes, so he left the shelter and continued his search.

The second time, it struck without warning, slashing obliquely through the air. He looked up just before he was hit and raised his arm protectively. The falcon slashed his shirt and ripped at his skin, but he managed to beat it back.

Now, it had been five minutes since he had last seen the bird. He looked frequently at the sky, and whenever he saw it wheeling, he ducked into the shadows.

"Angela! Angela!"

As usual, no response.

Looking down at the ground, he saw blood, blue-black in moonlight. For a moment, he thought it was his own, but no—the spattered drops led him forward in a neat line.

Whose blood? Angela's? The professor's?

He followed the trail, pausing frequently to listen. The professor might still be alive, and might still have his gun. But he heard nothing as he went.

Eventually, he came to the Patio de los Arrayánes, with the broad, placid central pool. At the far end of the court, he saw a body floating in the water, drifting gently. There were silver clouds reflected in the pool. It was a horrible scene.

He stood for a long moment, and then a figure emerged from the shadows at the far end.

"Angela."

She nodded, her body shaking.

He ran toward her.

As he approached, the falcon swooped down once more and struck her full in the face. The still evening was broken by the most horrible scream he had ever heard. The bird clung to her face, and she struggled briefly, trying to beat it away. Her shrieks mingled with the cries of the bird, and the beating of powerful wings.

Then the bird climbed back toward the sky, and Angela crumpled to the ground.

Even from a distance, he could see the terrible slashes down her face and the deep bleeding gash at the base of her neck.

23. THE REAL THING

He ran forward. When he reached her, she was no longer breathing, no longer moving. Nearby, the professor's gun lay beside the pool; Ross picked it up and stuck it in his belt. If the bird returned, at least he would have some defense.

He bent over Angela, feeling his emotions twist inside him. He lifted her head, now a dead weight in his hands. He caressed her black hair, stroked her cheek.

And stopped.

I am going insane, he thought.

He looked at the body in the pool, the moon in the sky, and the circling bird. He looked back at Angela and touched her cheek once more.

There could be no doubt. Roughness.

A beard.

He tugged at the hair, and it came away in his hands to reveal close-cropped blond hair. He smeared the make-up with his fingers, wiping it away, and plucked off the false eyelashes.

Jackman.

The professor's assistant.

When had they made the switch?

And where was Angela?

With a high-pitched shriek, the falcon dived again. Ross looked up, saw it coming, dropped the gun, and jumped into the pool. It was not deep, but deep enough. He hoped to hell falcons would not go into water. He stayed under, holding his breath as long as he could, and then surfaced.

The body of the professor was floating alongside him. And high above, the falcon still circled, gliding in slow smooth arcs, its shadow passing over the pool, the courtyard, the sloping roofs of the palace.

Ross struggled out of the water. The cold air struck him; he shivered. The cuts on his arm stung. He picked up the gun and opened it, checking the magazine. Five shots left.

So be it, he thought, and snapped it shut again. Five shots would be enough, if he were lucky. And if he were not lucky, it wouldn't matter anyway.

He thought again about Angela. She had been switched for Jackman—when? He cast his mind back over the last two hours and decided it must have been while he and the professor were in the hole with the rats.

Once they came up, Angela had hardly spoken—maybe two words, and those in a whisper. He hadn't noticed it at the time, but now he remembered. And she had kept her back turned to him, most of the time.

So she must be somewhere near the fortress. And probably Karin Brenner was with her.

Shivering, dripping water, he headed back toward the hole. He dodged from building to building, keeping in the shadows, always watching for the falcon. It was slow, cautious progress, but eventually he found himself overlooking the courtyard of the fort. It was large and brightly lit under the moon. He could never cross it without getting hit by the bird. He would have to go around.

But how?

He looked, eyes straining in the darkness. A path led around the walls to the right. The trees and bushes were fairly dense; he would have a chance if he went that way.

He set out.

He was tired and shivering constantly. Fatigue made him slow and sloppy. He moved painfully, stopping frequently to catch his breath.

And always, high above, the falcon.

At length, he had circled around the courtyard and was able to climb through a hole in the wall to reach the stoneworks inside. Off to his right was a tower; nearby, the remnants of barracks.

"Angela!"

He listened and heard nothing but the wind. And then, something else: a high-pitched whine, like a trapped animal.

"Angela!"

The sound was clearer, louder, encouraged by his voice. He realized suddenly that it was coming from the tower. Looking up, he saw that the tower was reached by a series of exposed steps, perhaps twenty in all. While he was climbing them, he would be easy prey for the falcon.

And then he saw something else in the moonlight. A woman, lying across the steps, near the top. For a horrified moment, he thought it was Angela, and then he saw it was not: Karin Brenner.

Her blonde hair blew lifelessly in the wind.

Listening, he heard the sound from the tower again. Angela was still there, and still alive. He crawled around the perimeter of the fortress to a good vantage point near the steps. He removed his gun and waited. The falcon was circling near the fortress. He waited until it moved off, farther away. Then he scrambled up the steps, two at a time. The bird saw him, came back, and streaked down toward him. He leaped over the body of Karin and flung himself through the open door into the tower just as the falcon whooshed past him.

He paused, looked back, and watched the bird circle around for a second try. It moved with a powerful grace, climbing, lifting, coming around.

A sound inside the tower distracted him. He looked back and saw Angela lying on the stone, tied and gagged with tape. She was wearing her bra and panties.

He pulled the tape away from her mouth and freed her hands.

"My God," she said, "what's happened to you?" She touched the long tears in his shirt and the blood.

"That damned bird," he said, cutting her ankles free.

"What bird?"

"The falcon," he said, and then stopped. She had a puzzled look on her face. "When did you—"

"While you were down in the hole," she said. "Karin and Jackman got me. He dressed in my clothes. It was in case the emerald wasn't down there. They were going to make you think he was me so that you'd tell him where the stone was."

"Clever," Ross said, helping her up.

"Where are they now?"

"Dead. All of them. Jackman, the professor, and Karin, too—right outside."

Angela shivered and rubbed her wrists. "How?"

"There's a trained falcon out there."

"It must be the count," she said. "He keeps a whole roost of them."

"Great," Ross said. He should have known from the start.

"Karin was guarding me," Angela said in a low voice. "I heard a scream, but—"

At that moment, the falcon swooped past the outside, giving a shrill cry. Angela froze.

"Is that it?"

"Yes," Ross said. "That's it. Terrifically keen eyesight. He seems to find us unerringly." He looked at her. "We've got to get out of here, but you can't leave like that. What about clothes?"

"Jackman's are over there."

Ross picked up a shirt and trousers. "They'll fit if you roll up the cuffs and sleeves."

She began to dress quickly. He watched her and thought of the body floating in the pool. He went over and kissed her lightly on the back of the neck as she was buckling the trousers.

"What was that for?" she said.

"Old times' sake," he said.

Outside, the falcon made another pass with a flapping rush of wings.

"Where are we going now?" she said.

"To the Court of Lions. To get the real stone."

She was stuffing the shirt into the pants. "Where's the count?"

"I don't know," Ross said. "But he can't be far."

She finished dressing and turned to him.

"How do I look?"

"Great. Come on."

He took her to the door, and pointed down the steps. The falcon was above, circling lazily high in the sky.

"We've got to get down. At the bottom, there's a protected place, but you're exposed on the steps. We'll have to run for it. You go first; I'll cover you. But move fast."

"All right."

She paused for a moment, looking up at the bird. Then she ran, her shoes clattering on the steps. Ross watched the falcon tensely, glanced down at her, then up to the falcon again.

The bird did not seem to notice. It circled lazily, apparently unaware of the people below.

When she had reached the bottom and ducked back into the shadows, he called, "You all right?"

"Yes. Come on."

Ross sprinted down.

The bird attacked, careening down from the sky. Ross fired at it, missed, and the falcon veered away. He fell the last few steps, tumbling to the ground, and picked himself up. He dodged into the darkness.

"I don't get it," he said. "That damned falcon didn't pay any attention to you."

Angela frowned, and sniffed. "You know," she said, "you smell funny."

"Sweat, I imagine. I'm scared, baby."

She shook her head. "Something else."

"It must be—"

"The insect spray."

He snapped his fingers. "Of course! All four of us were sprayed—the professor, Karin, me, and you. Jackman wasn't, but he wore your clothes, so he got attacked…"

Quickly, he stripped off his shirt.

"What are you doing?"

"A little test."

He waited until the bird was overhead, then threw his shirt out into the courtyard. The cloth never reached the ground. The falcon was on it in a flash, gripping, tearing, shredding with its beak. It carried the shirt high into the sky and then, apparently bored, dropped it.

"There it is," Ross said.

"It's awful," Angela said, shuddering.

"Five hundred varieties of cologne," Ross said grimly. "And this bird is keyed to one of them. Pretty." He ran out to the courtyard and picked up the shirt.

"What are you doing?"

"I need it."

"Leave it there."

"No. I must have it."

"But why?"

"You'll see. Now let's find those lions."

It took nearly an hour to find their way. Ross was convinced that the count and Joaquim were already in the Alhambra, or soon would be. He moved forward cautiously, cold, with his shirt rolled up under his arm. They reached the Court of Lions at three in the morning, just as the sky was beginning to lighten faintly, and a slight mist hung low to the ground.

They were alone.

"All right. Now we'll see. You wait here."

Ross ran forward, crouched in the moonlight, until he reached the base of the fountain. He clicked his light on. Water from the fountains sprayed all around him as he crawled beneath the slimy underside of the basin and began his search.

It was surprisingly easy. He found it in a matter of seconds, a metal box wedged under the fountain, behind the rump of one lion. He opened it and found cotton; beneath that, another emerald pyramid.

Only this time it was real.

With the spray and gurgling water all around him, he flicked on his light to examine the stone. It was precisely cut and beautifully polished, and seemed to weigh more than a pound. It seemed to glow in the light of his torch.

"Angela," he said. "I've got it. This is it."

There was a short pause, and then a rasping, familiar mechanical voice said, "And we have her, Dr. Ross. Would you care to trade?"

He peered forward into the darkness but could see nothing. "Who's that? Joaquim?"

The rasping voice gave a laugh.

"Where's the count?"

"Right here, Doctor," said a high voice.

"Is Angela all right?"

"Tell him, my dear," said the count.

"Yes," Angela said. "I'm all right, Pete."

Ross was frightened, and cold, and tired. It took him a moment to gather his wits. He had an advantage, perhaps more than one.

"All right," he called into the darkness. "Now listen to me. I have the emerald. Do you understand? I have the real one, not the fake."

"We are well aware of that," the count said.

"If you want to get it in one piece, let the girl go. Otherwise, I'll smash the emerald."

The count laughed. "You don't seem to understand, Doctor. Not at all. Unless you hand over the emerald within one minute, we will kill this pretty young thing."

So it was like that. Ross sighed; Angela was right, he was innocent and naïve. He thought furiously, his mind churning, examining possibilities, alternatives. Innocent, too innocent. Why not use that? Make it work for him? "Are you serious about a trade?" he asked. "A fair trade?"

"Of course, Doctor. I am a man of honor."

"All right, then. Send Angela forward, toward me. I'll wrap the emerald in my shirt so it won't be damaged and toss it out to you." He paused. "I have a gun," he said, "so be careful."

"Oh, I am sure you are an excellent shot," the count chuckled.

There was a pause. "Is it a deal?" Ross said.

"Yes. A deal."

"No tricks?"

"No tricks."

"Then send the girl out."

There was a moment's pause, and Angela stepped, frightened, out into the moonlit courtyard. In the shadows, he tried to see the count and Joaquim, but could not.

"There she is, Doctor. Now the stone."

"All right."

He wrapped it swiftly in his shirt.

"Here you are." He tossed the bundle out. It landed softly.

"How do we know it's really the emerald?"

"You'll have to come out and check."

"Then you might shoot us," the count said.

"Yes. And you might shoot the girl."

The count gave another laugh. "You learn fast, Doctor."

"I'm still young."

"So it seems. All right: I will check it."

"When you do," Ross said, "make sure you stay in sight until Angela and I have left."

"As you wish."

Ross glanced over at Angela. She was standing rigidly, waiting. A moment later, the count emerged from the shadows, wearing his cape, moving forward toward the bundle.

Ross caught his breath. Anything might happen. But it was certain to be swift.

The count, chuckling to himself, bent over the bundle, lifted it up, and began to unwrap it.

Then he froze.

He smelled it, and knew what it meant.

"You bastard," the count said.

"Run, Angela!" Ross shouted.

And the falcon struck.

The little man was knocked down easily by the bird, which clawed at his fallen body. The count shrieked horribly, and from the shadows, Joaquim began to fire. Ross saw the spurts of flame from the machine gun. Joaquim was shooting at the bird.

Ross took aim and shot Joaquim twice. The machine gun went silent. He looked back at the count. The bird was dead, a trembling mass of feathers, twitching on the ground. The count, however, did not move. He lay on his back, arms flung over his face protectively.

And he did not move.

Alongside him, shining in the moonlight, was the emerald.

24. THE FAITHFUL SERVANT

Ross waited several moments, then said, "Angela, you all right?"

In a whisper, from behind him: "Yes."

"Good. Stay there. I'm going to get the emerald."

He crawled out from beneath the fountain and grinned. "Not bad for a guy who never fired a gun before, eh?"

He started for the emerald, lying near the body of the count. He reached for it, picked it up.

Then the gun opened up.

He acted instinctively, falling to the ground, then rolling back toward the fountain. All around him, tufts of dirt were kicked up into the air. From the fountain, he ran, zigzagging toward the shadows where he thought Angela would be.

He hesitated, panting, in the darkness.

"Pete? Is that you?"

He moved toward the voice. "Yes."

"Who's shooting?"

"It must be Joaquim."

"I thought he was dead."

"So did I." A thought occurred to him. "Those shots, just now. Were they from a machine gun?"

"No," she said.

"Perhaps it's jammed."

"Or he's wounded. They are hard to fire with one hand."

There was a pause.

"Now what?" he said.

"Now, I kill you," rasped a voice from across the court-yard.

"Good luck," Ross said, flinging the answer back.

"Shhh," Angela said. "He wants you to talk so he can locate the voices."

Ross cursed his own stupidity. An innocent to the last, he thought.

He looked out at the court, at the bodies of the falcon and the count.

"You have the stone?"

"Yes. What time is it?"

"Almost four."

"When's sunrise?"

"Here on the mountain, around five."

"Well, when it's light, the police will come. Perhaps they've already been attracted by the gunshots."

"No. Joaquim will not wait. He will try to kill us before that. He is desperate."

"So am I," Ross said, gripping the emerald tightly in his hand.

"How many bullets are left?"

He opened his clip and felt the shells in the darkness. "Two."

"That's bad," she said.

They waited for a moment in silence.

Across the court, Joaquim gave a low, harsh laugh. It floated across the stillness toward them, the laugh of a monster.

"He's terribly strong," she said.

"What are you trying to do, encourage me?"

"Let's leave," she said.

Ross thought. "No," he said.

"But we must. With only two bullets…"

"I'm leaving here," he said, "alone."

"No. You can't."

"If you come, you'll get killed."

"I will go wherever you go."

"No," he said. "I know where I can get another weapon, but I can only make it alone. All right?"

"Another weapon? A gun?"

"Yes. Now sit tight."

Another unearthly laugh drifted over toward them, and then a thick cough.

"He's not in good shape. He may be dying already," Ross said.

"You can't be sure of that."

"I know," he said, "but it's our only chance." He put his hand on her shoulder. "Now listen. Stay here, quietly, and wait. I'll be back in a few minutes. But promise me you'll stay."

"I promise."

"Whatever happens, don't make a sound."

She sighed. "All right."

Ross stood up, holding the emerald in the hand which was bandaged by the doctor. In his other hand he held the gun. He took a deep breath and called loudly, "Joaquim!"

A harsh laugh came back.

"Listen to me. The game is up. I've got the emerald, and I'm leaving. The police will be here within five minutes. If you try to follow me, I'll kill you. Understand?"

Four shots whistled around him.

He began to run.

Apparently, Joaquim followed the sound of his footsteps. Succeeding shots were very close; once, a chip of plaster struck Ross in the face, stinging and cutting. He did not break stride but ran for the doorway and out. There he paused, getting his bearings, and ran south, through gardens. The sky was beginning to lighten now, and the gardens were no longer so comfortably dark.

Behind him, he heard Joaquim. Three bullets snapped through the trees.

He ran as fast as he could, hoping he was going in the right direction. One shot passed so close to his elbow that he felt the heated air of its passage.

A good man, Joaquim. The faithful servant, even to the end.

Two more shots. One plucked at his trousers. It was too close: Ross abruptly turned off to one side, scrambling through the bushes, up along a small garden courtyard. Joaquim heard the sound and fired into the foliage, but he was nowhere near.

Ross moved back, retracing his steps, until he could look down over the brick path along which Joaquim must come. Ross gripped the emerald in his bandaged, aching hand and held the gun straight ahead.

For a long time, there was no sound, no movement. Joaquim was waiting somewhere in the gardens. Ross held his breath. A few yards away, a small bird fluttered down onto a branch. Joaquim fired, cracking the wood of the tree.

Ross waited.

It seemed an eternity, with nothing but a gentle early morning breeze. But he knew that Joaquim must act soon; with every passing minute, the sky became lighter. Soon the guards would arrive, and the maintenance men, and then the tourists.

Ross checked his watch.

It occurred to him that Joaquim had gone back for Angela; he considered it, and pushed the thought from his mind. Joaquim would not bother, because he knew Ross had the emerald.

Or did he know?

In his mind, he saw Joaquim returning to the Court of Lions and finding Angela huddled there. It would be a brief meeting, no hesitation, no regrets, a single bullet in the head…

At that moment, he heard a sound. The sound of a shoe scraping on stone.

Ross raised his gun.

Joaquim appeared, moving out from the bushes, no more than ten yards from where Ross lay hidden. With a shock, Ross saw that he was uninjured; the big man moved slowly, strongly, looking around him.

Ross took aim and fired.

He knew as he fired that Joaquim was hit; he watched as he spun away with the force of the bullet and fell to his stomach on the ground. He fell very hard and did not move.

Ross waited. He watched the body carefully for any sign of movement. There was none. He tried to see where he had hit Joaquim, but could not. However, after a moment, a thin trickle of blood seeped across the stone from beneath the body.

Still, it might be a superficial wound. Ross hesitated, then fired again, aiming for the head or chest. He struck the leg and watched it kick away.

The rest of the body did not move. There was no sound.

Only a dead man, he thought, could take a bullet in the leg that way.

Ross moved out of the bushes, holding his empty gun loosely in his hand. He approached the body, and suddenly, Joaquim spun and raised his own gun.

"Hold it," Ross said.

Joaquim did not move, but watched Ross closely.

"Don't move a muscle," Ross said. He held the gun in front

of him, acutely aware that it was empty, that it was a monstrous bluff. But he could see the uncertainty and the fear in Joaquim's eyes.

Ross stopped and backed off two steps. "I don't want to kill you," Ross said. "Don't make me."

His words sounded ridiculous to him. His voice was trembling and unconvincing.

"You know," Joaquim said, "I don't believe you have bullets left."

"There is one way to find out," Ross said, taking another step back.

"Yes," Joaquim said.

In a swift movement, he raised his own gun and fired. Ross turned and ran, dodging back into the bushes and then away toward the courtyard near the fortress. He heard Joaquim grunt in pain as he raised himself to his feet.

Two more shots.

And then it happened. A bullet struck his hand, shattering the emerald, crumbling it to powder. The force of the shell lifted his arm high, swinging it up. Ross closed his fist on a handful of splinters and dust.

Joaquim was still after him.

Ross ran. He scrambled down the steps to the courtyard, moving to the interior court. He knew without looking back that Joaquim was following. Up ahead, he saw the gaping hole from the construction. His hand stung fiercely; there were jagged splinters in the bandages.

On the ground he saw the tank and the gas masks. He scooped them up and jumped down the hole without looking. He landed in a cloud of thick choking dust. It was very dark; only the faintest light filtered down through the hole.

He pulled one of the masks over his face and ran deep into

one of the passages. He threw the second mask away but lugged the tank with him. It clanged against the rocks as he ran. He finally set it down, crawled behind a wall, and waited.

Around him, in the darkness, he could hear the squeaking and rustling of rats. For a long time, there was nothing else, and then a single, quiet thud: Joaquim had jumped down.

From behind the wall, Ross could look down the passage toward the hole. There was enough light to see Joaquim, huge and lumbering, standing in a cloud of gray dust. Joaquim still held his gun; he looked around in a slow, almost lazy way.

"Doctor?" The rasping voice was amused, toying. If Joaquim was in pain, he gave no sign.

Ross said nothing.

"You will never escape alive, Doctor."

Ross bit his lip, smelled the rubber of the gas mask.

"I will kill you. I have vowed it."

Slowly, Ross stretched the nozzle forward from the tank and turned on the gas. It hissed out softly.

He waited. Joaquim started off in another direction.

"Over here, Joaquim."

His voice echoed through the underground chambers, but Joaquim had fixed the direction well: four bullets spanged off the rocks around him. A light was flicked on, and it played around the room.

Ross ducked back, cursing the way he had wasted his last bullets. The light swung past his hiding place.

"I am presenting an excellent target, Doctor," Joaquim said. "Do you wish to try your luck?"

Ross did not move.

"Or is it that you have no more ammunition?"

He laughed. The harsh voice echoed through the chambers.

"Come and get me," Ross said.

The light came back on. The beam swung in a slow arc, stopping occasionally. Ross heard the sound of Joaquim's footsteps coming closer. He heard the hiss of the gas. Peering around the corner, he saw the light of the torch and, vaguely, the outlines of the huge body.

Joaquim stepped closer and closer. He was now only ten feet away. The gas was hissing out, but it had no effect.

It wasn't going to work.

Ross realized that he had turned the nozzle too low; the gas concentration was insufficient. Joaquim was practically standing on the tank, and coming closer with each step. And yet nothing was happening.

One chance.

One in a thousand.

Ross waited until the light moved away, then bent over and picked up the heavy cylinder. He threw it off to one side of Joaquim.

"Here, Joaquim!"

The big man fired instinctively.

The tank was punctured, and clouds of milky vapor spurted upward. Ross had a glimpse of him as he clutched his face and his throat, gasping, making ghastly raw sounds. Then he toppled and fell into the clouds of gas and was hidden.

Ross pressed his mask tight against his face and climbed out of the hole.

25. THE WAY OUT

He found Angela standing over the hole as he came out. She helped him up and said, "What happened?"

"Joaquim's dead."

"Gas?"

Small wispy vapors were rising from the hole into the morning light.

"Yes. Gas."

He pulled the mask off his head, and she touched his face, which was bathed in sweat. She kissed him lightly and threw the mask back down the hole.

"Let's get out of here," he said.

They crawled over the main gates, past a sleeping guard, and moved down the mountainside to where their car was parked in a dark glade of trees. His hand throbbed; she helped him into the car and got in behind the wheel.

They started down the mountain.

"You've got to see a doctor," she said.

"Yes."

"We'll go to the same one."

"That poor fellow," Ross said.

As she drove, her black hair tugged by the wind, she smiled at him and said, "Well, at least it's over."

"Yes, it is."

"We can leave now."

"I'd like that," Ross said.

"Where would you like to go? I was thinking of Paris, myself."

"I've just been to Paris," he said. "How about Rome?"

"Too hot."

"Then Capri."

She smiled. "All right, Capri."

He leaned over and kissed her cheek as she drove.

"I like you," he said.

"You say that to all the girls," she said, and smiled.

She drove on for a few minutes in silence, then said, "We can leave tomorrow, first thing."

"Why not today?"

"Well, we have to go back."

"What for?"

"The emerald, of course," she said. "You don't have it with you. By the way, where did you hide it?"

"I didn't," he said.

"Pete, come on, don't kid—"

"Really, I didn't."

"Darling—"

"Angela, really, I didn't hide it." He was frowning as he watched her.

Abruptly, she pulled over to the side of the road. She reached back behind the seat and produced a gun.

"Peter."

"Angela, for Christ's sake." He was tired; this was silly; his hand ached miserably.

"Peter. Tell me."

He felt suddenly foolish again, innocent and foolish and unsuspecting. Her face was set and hard behind the barrel of the gun.

"Is that thing loaded?"

"Peter, don't play games with me. I want that emerald."

"I haven't got it."

"You must. You had it when you left the Court of Lions."

Her features were twisted in a way he had not seen before. She was no longer beautiful to him; everything was wrong; everything was changed.

"Not anymore."

She shook her head and waved the gun at him.

"Tell me," he said. "Would you kill me?"

"If I had to."

"And if I told you where the emerald was?"

"Then I would go off with you to Capri, and we would be very happy together."

"Uh-huh."

She said, "Peter, I'm serious, I want that stone."

He raised his bandaged hand and opened it up to her.

"All right," he said. "Take it."

She looked at the hand and saw the greenish dust and the green splinters. It took her a moment to realize what it meant.

"Joaquim," Ross said softly, "was a very good shot."

As a last try, she said, "You're lying."

"No," he said. "Now take me to a doctor and shut up."

In front of the doctor's home, in the early reddish light, he got out of the car, shut the door, and looked down at her.

"Well," he said, "it was fun."

She smiled slightly. "In a way."

"Yes," he said, nodding. "In a way."

Then she slammed the car in gear and roared off, down the quiet early-morning streets of Granada, and he had a last glimpse of her black hair and her shoulders set hard as she spun the wheel and disappeared around the corner, and out of sight.

EPILOGUE

The mandible was broken across the ramus. Five teeth were knocked out, and three were displaced. There was a hairline fracture along the right zygomatic arch.

Peter Ross sat in the dark X-ray reading room on the seventh floor and looked back over his shoulder at Jackson, the plastic surgeon.

"Nasty," Ross said. "Who is it?"

"Some drunk. Got into a fight with a couple of sailors who tried to kick his head in."

"You going to do him now?"

Jackson sighed. It was midnight, and he was tired. "Yes, I guess so. The bastard is groaning something awful."

Ross nodded and pulled the X-rays down from the lighted board. "Good luck."

Jackson said, "How was your trip?"

"Fine."

"You have a hell of a tan. All rested up?"

"Yes. All rested."

Jackson laughed. "Don't kid me. All you did is drink and screw for a month."

Ross smiled. "Yes, but you know, it gets boring after a while."

"Is that why you came back early?"

"Yes."

"That's the trouble with medicine," Jackson said. "You get so you can't relax. You get so that even on vacation, you can't have a good time."

"I know," Ross said, "just what you mean."

VIDEO INTERVIEW

In the living room of the house, Todd put the video camera down and stared at his grandfather. "How could you do this?" he said. "I needed you to be serious. This is for school."

"I was serious."

"It's an assignment." Todd shook his head. "We're graded."

"What's wrong?"

"Grandpa," the boy said, "nobody will believe that crazy story. A Spanish count? A huge emerald from Montezuma? Running around Granada all night? Isn't that like a museum or something? I'll say one thing, you got a real imagination."

Peter Ross sighed. "I've never told the full story to anyone before. Not even your father."

"I can believe that," Todd said, packing up his equipment. "If I were you, I'd never tell it again. 'Cause it makes you look silly."

Ross sighed again. "Nobody believed me back then, either."

Todd wound the electrical cord for the camera. "Just promise me," he said, "never say anything about this story around my friends, okay? I mean, just never mention it."

"Okay," he said.

"I'd never hear the end of it." He opened the video camera, removed the DVD, put it on the table. "I have no use for this." He turned to go. "You promise never to mention this story?"

"Yes, Todd," he said.

"Okay, then," his grandson said, and went outside. Peter Ross watched him go, then got out of the chair in the living room, and walked to the table. He picked up the DVD, went to his office, and opened the bottom drawer of his desk. Inside was an old blue passport from the 1960s, its corner clipped when it expired. He opened it now, looking at the absurdly young face in the photograph, and noticing the traces of fine greenish powder in the creases of the passport.

After a long moment, Peter Ross put the passport back, and the DVD beside it, and closed the drawer again. Then he went outside, to see what the young people were doing.

Los Angeles: 5 a.m. PDT
Hour 12

The gray government sedan was waiting in a deserted corner of Los Angeles International Airport. Seen from the air, it cast a long shadow across the concrete runway in the pale morning light. He watched the sedan as his helicopter descended and landed a short distance from the car.

The driver came running up, bent over beneath the spinning blades, and opened the door. A gust of warm, dry August air swirled into the interior of the helicopter.

"Mr. Graves?"

"That's right."

"Come with me please."

Graves got out, carrying his briefcase, and walked to the car. He climbed into the back seat and they drove off away from the runway toward the freeway.

"Do you know where we're going?" Graves asked.

The driver consulted a clipboard. "One-oh-one-three-one Washington, Culver City, I have."

"I think that's right." Graves settled back in the seat. California numbering: he'd never get used to it. It was as bad as a zip code. He opened his early edition of the *New York Times* and tried to read it. He had tried on the helicopter but had found it impossible to concentrate. He assumed that was because of the noise. And the distractions: when they passed over San Clemente, halfway between Los Angeles and San Diego, he had been craning his neck, peering out the window like an ordinary tourist. The President was there now, had been for the last week.

He looked at the headlines: trouble in the UN, arguments in the German parliament about the mark, Britain and France squabbling… He put the paper aside and stared out the window at Los Angeles, flat and bleak in the early morning light.

"Good trip, sir?" the driver asked. It was perfectly said— no inflection, no prying, just detached polite interest. The driver didn't know who Graves was. He didn't know where he had come from. He didn't know what his business was. All the driver knew was that Graves was important enough to have a government helicopter fly him in and a government sedan pick him up.

"Fine, thanks." Graves smiled, staring out the window. In fact the trip had been horrible. Phelps had called him just an hour before and asked him to come up and give a briefing on Wright. That was the way Phelps worked—everything was a crisis, there were no routine activities. It was typical that Phelps hadn't bothered to let Graves know beforehand that he was even in Los Angeles.

Although on reflection, Graves knew he should have expected that. With the Republican Convention in San Diego, all the activity of the country had shifted from Washington to the West Coast. The President was in the Western White House in San Clemente; the Convention was 80 miles to the south; and Phelps—what would Phelps do? Obviously, relocate discreetly in the nearest large city, which was Los Angeles. As Graves considered it, Los Angeles became the inevitable choice.

Phelps needed the telephone lines for data transmission. It was as simple as that. L.A. was the third largest city in America, and it would have plenty of telephone lines that the Department of State (Intelligence Division) could take over on short notice. It was inevitable.

"Here we are, sir," the driver said, pulling over to the curb. He got out and opened the door for Graves. "Am I to wait for you, sir?"

"Yes, I think so."

"Very good, sir."

Graves paused and looked up at the building. It was a rather ordinary four-story office building in an area of Los Angeles that seemed almost a slum. The building, not particularly new, was outstandingly ugly. And the paint was flaking away from the facade.

Graves walked up the steps and entered the lobby. As he went through the doors he looked at his watch. It was exactly 5 A.M. Phelps was waiting for him in the deserted lobby. Phelps wore a lightweight glen-plaid suit and a worried expression. He shook hands with Graves and said, "How was your flight?" His voice echoed slightly in the lobby.

"Fine," Graves said.

They walked to the elevators, passing the ground-floor offices, which seemed mostly devoted to a bank.

"Like this place?" Phelps said.

"Not much."

"It was the best we could find on short notice," he said.

A guard with a sign-in book stood in front of the elevators. Graves let Phelps sign first; then he took the pen and wrote his name, his authorization, and the time. He saw that Decker and Venn were already there.

They got onto the elevator and pressed the button for the

third floor. "Decker and Venn are already here," Phelps said.

"I saw."

Phelps nodded and smiled, as much as he ever smiled. "I keep forgetting about you and your powers of observation."

"I keep forgetting about you, too," Graves said.

Phelps ignored the remark. "I've planned two meetings for today," he said. "You've got the briefing in an hour—Wilson, Peckham, and a couple of others. But I think you should hear about Sigma Station first."

"All right," Graves said. He didn't know what the hell Phelps was talking about, but he wasn't going to give him the satisfaction of asking.

They got off at the third floor and walked past some peeling posters of Milan and Tahiti and through a small typing pool, the desks now deserted, the typewriters neatly covered.

"What is this place?" Graves said.

"Travel agency," Phelps said. "They went out of business but they had a lot of—"

"Telephone lines."

"Yes. We took over the floor."

"How long you planning to stay?" Graves asked. There was an edge to his voice that he didn't bother to conceal. Phelps knew how he felt about the Department.

"Just through the Convention," Phelps said, with elaborate innocence. "What did you think?"

"I thought it might be permanent."

"Good Lord, no. Why would we do a thing like that?"

"I can't imagine," Graves said.

Past the typing pool they came to a section of private offices. The walls were painted an institutional beige. It reminded Graves of a prison, or a hospital. No wonder the travel agency went out of business, he thought.

"I know how you feel," Phelps said.

"Do you?" Graves asked.

"Yes. You're…ambivalent about the section."

"I'm ambivalent about the domestic activities."

"We all are," Phelps said. He said it easily, in the smooth, oil-on-the-waters manner that he had perfected. And his father before him. Phelps's father had been an undersecretary of state during the Roosevelt administration. Phelps himself was a product of the Dalton School, Andover, Yale, and Harvard Law School. If he sat still, ivy would sprout from his ears. But he never sat still.

"How do you find San Diego?" he asked, walking along with his maddeningly springy step.

"Boring and hot."

Phelps sighed. "Don't blame me. *I* didn't choose it."

Graves did not reply. They continued down a corridor and came upon a guard, who nodded to Phelps. "Good morning, Mr. Phelps." And to Graves: "Good morning, sir." Phelps flashed his pink card; so did Graves. The guard allowed them to pass further down the corridor past a large banner that read FIRST CLASS SERVICE ON COACH.

"You've got a guard already," Graves said.

"There's a lot of expensive equipment to look after," Phelps said. They made a right turn and entered a conference room.

There were just four of them: Graves; Phelps, looking springy and alert as he greeted everyone; Decker, who was thin and dark, intense-looking; and Venn, who was nearly fifty, graying, sloppy in his dress. Graves had never met Decker or Venn before, but he knew they were both scientists. They were too academic and too uncomfortable to be anything else.

Phelps ran the meeting. "This is John Graves, who is the

world's foremost expert on John Wright." He smiled slightly. "Mr. Graves has plenty of background, so you can speak as technically as you want. Decker, why don't you begin."

Decker cleared his throat and opened a briefcase in front of him, removing a sheaf of computer printout. He slipped through the green pages as he spoke. "I've been working in Special Projects Division for the last six months," he said. "I was assigned to establish redundancy programs on certain limited-access files so that we could check call-up locations to these data banks, which are mostly located in Arlington Hall in Washington."

He paused and glanced at Graves to see if the information was making sense. Graves nodded.

"The problem is basically one of access-line proliferation. A data bank is just a collection of information stored on magnetic tape drums. It can be anywhere in the country. To get information out of it, you need to hook into the main computer with an access substation. That can also be any-where in the country. Every major data bank has a large number of access substations. For limited or special-purpose access—stations that need to draw out information once or twice a week, let's say—we employ commercial telephone lines; we don't have our own lines. To tie in to a peripheral computer substation, you telephone a call number and hook your phone up to the computer terminal. That's it. As long as you have a half-duplex or full-duplex telephone line, you're in business."

Graves nodded. "How is the call number coded?"

"We'll come to that," Decker said, looking at Venn. "For now, we'll concentrate on the system. Some of the major data banks, like the ones held by Defense, may have five hundred or a thousand access lines. A year ago, Wilkens's congressional committee started to worry about unauthorized tapping into those access lines. In theory, a bright boy who knew computers could tap into the system and call out any information he wanted from the data banks. He could get all sorts of classified information."

Decker sighed. "So I was hired to install redundancy checks on the system. Echo checks, bit additions, that sort of thing. My job was to make sure we could verify which stations drew out information from the data banks, and what information they drew. I finished that work a month ago."

Graves glanced at Phelps. Phelps was watching them all intently, pretending he was following the discussion. Graves knew that it was over Phelps's head.

"Just before I finished," Decker said, "we discovered that an unauthorized station was tapping into the system. We called it Sigma Station, but we were unable to characterize it. By that I mean that we knew Sigma was drawing information, but we didn't know where, or how."

He flipped to a green sheet of computer printout and pushed it across the table to Graves. "Sigma is the underlined station. You can see that on this particular day, July 21, 1972, it tapped into the system at ten oh four p.m. Eastern time and maintained the contact for seven minutes; then it broke out. We determined that Sigma was tapping in at around ten o'clock two or three nights a week. But that was all we knew."

Decker turned to Venn, who said, "I came into the picture at this point. I'd been at Bell Labs working on telephone tracer mechanisms. The telephone company has a problem with unauthorized calls—calls verbally charged to a phony number, calls charged to a wrong credit card number, that kind of thing. I was working on a computer tracing system. Defense asked me to look at the Sigma Station problem."

"One ought to say," Phelps said, "that the data bank being tapped by Sigma was a Defense bank."

"Yes," Venn said. "It was a Defense bank. With two or three taps a week at about ten p.m. That was all I knew when I began. However, I made some simple assumptions. First, you've got to have a computer terminal in order to tap the system. That is, once you've called the number that links you to the computer, you must use a teletype-writing or CRT apparatus compatible with the Defense system."

"Are those terminals common?"

"No," Venn said. "They are quite advanced and fairly uncommon. I started with a list of them."

Graves nodded.

"Then I considered the timing. Ten p.m. Eastern time is seven p.m. in California, where most of these sophisticated terminals in defense industry applications are located. If an employee were illegally using a terminal to tap into Defense, he couldn't do it during office hours. On the other hand, it requires an extraordinary access to get into an East Coast terminal location at ten at night—or into a Midwest location at eight or nine. Therefore Sigma was probably on the West Coast."

"So you checked the West Coast terminals?"

"Yes. Because in order to hook into the Defense system, you'd have to unhook from your existing system. What corporation, R&D group, or production unit had a terminal that was unhooked at seven p.m. Western time twice a week? Answer: None. New question: What group had its terminals repaired twice a week? Repairing would entail unhooking. Answer: The Southern California Association of Insurance Underwriters, a company based in San Diego."

Graves said, "So you investigated the repairman and you found—"

"We found our man," Venn said, looking slightly annoyed with Graves. "His name is Timothy Drew. He has been doing repair work on the S.C. Association computers for about six weeks. It turns out nobody authorized those repairs; he just showed up and—"

"But you haven't picked him up."

Phelps coughed. "No, actually. We haven't picked him up yet because he's—"

"Disappeared," Graves said.

"That's right," Phelps said. "How did you know?"

"Tim Drew is a friend of John Wright. He's had dinner with him several times a week for the last month or so." As he spoke, Graves had a mental image of Drew—early thirties, blond-looking, muscular. Graves had run a check on him some weeks back and had discovered only that Drew was an ex-Army lieutenant, discharged one year before. A clean record in computer work, nothing good, nothing bad.

"We weren't able to find him," Venn said, "but we're still looking. We thought—"

Graves said, "There's only one thing I want to know. What information did Drew tap from the classified files?"

There was a long silence around the table. Finally Decker said, "We don't know."

"You don't know?" Graves lit a cigarette. "But that's the most important question—"

"Let me explain," Decker said. "Drew was an ex-Army officer with knowledge of computer systems. He knew that he couldn't call in on any old number. The call-in numbers are changed at irregular intervals, roughly once a week. But the possible permutations of the call-in number aren't great. With trial and error, he might have found it."

"You know he found the number," Graves said, "because you know he tapped in. The question is, what did he tap *out* from the system?"

"Well, once he was hooked up, he still had a problem. You

need subroutine codes to extract various kinds of information, and—"

"How often are the codes changed?"

"Not very often."

Graves found himself getting impatient. "How often are the codes changed?"

"About once a year."

Graves sighed. "So Drew might have used his old codes to get what he wanted?"

"Yes."

"Then we want to know what codes he knew. What sort of work did Drew do when he was in the Army?"

"He did topological work. Surface configurations, shipment routings, that sort of thing."

Graves glanced at Phelps. "Can we be more specific?"

"I'm afraid not," Phelps said. "Defense is unwilling to release Drew's work record to us. Defense is a little defensive, you might say, about the fact that this tap occurred in the first place."

There was a long silence. Graves stared at the men around the table. There were times, he thought, when working for the government was an exercise in total stupidity. Finally he said, "How can you get Defense to release the information?"

"I'm not sure we can," Phelps said. "But one of the reasons you're being briefed is that we were hoping you might be able to shed light on the situation."

"I might?"

"Yes. Drew was working for Wright, after all."

Before Graves could answer, the telephone rang. Phelps answered it, and said, "Yes, thank you," and hung up. He looked at Graves. "Do you have any thoughts about this?"

"None," Graves said.

"None at all?"

"None at all."

"Well," Phelps said, "perhaps something will occur to you in the next hour." He gave Graves a heavily disapproving look, then stood up and turned to Decker and Venn. "Thank you, gentlemen," he said. And to Graves: "Let's go."